CALL ME YUBBIE

Published by:
Apex Performance Solutions, LLC
467 Springdale Road
Westfield, MA 01085
413.562.2299
www.apexperformancesolutions.com

ISBN-13: 978-0-9824519-0-8
$12.95

Printed in the USA

Cover and book design
by Gwyn Kennedy Snider

CALL ME YUBBIE

ACKNOWLEDGEMENTS

With each venture in life, our success is predicated on the contributions that others make in helping us achieve our goal. One of life's most important lessons is that no man stands alone. Thus,I give recognition to those who have helped me accomplish this important undertaking.

My partner, best friend, and wife Deb continues to be patient with my endeavors. Her support has been instrumental. In over thirty years of marriage she has been involved in each of my undertakings. Her gentle spirit guides me through tough times and has given me valuable nurturing that inspired me and enabled me to achieve my goals. She has dedicated countless hours to editing this project and helping me deliver this valuable message.

It is said "all you need will be sent your way when you have mentally decided the outcome of your endeavor." I had an important message to deliver to our society on the impact of childhood bullying on our adult lives. I thought that my first book, *YUBBIE: THE FALL AND RISE OF AN EVERYDAY JOE,* was the means to accomplish my objective. Little did I know at the time that there was much more work to be done. Antoinette Kurtz encouraged me to pursue this writing endeavor despite the work ahead of me. It was her continuous support, editing, and positive reactions to my material that led to the success of this project. Antoinette and her team at *STRATEGIES* have been instrumental in helping me deliver this vital message through my workbooks and presentations.

Special mention and appreciation also must be extended to Tina Dunlop for her contribution to this project and to Deborah Halverson for her exceptional guidance and editing skills. Their input on this project has elevated its quality and success.

Journal Entry 1 - June 23

Waking up this morning, I thought it would be a great day. The first day of summer vacation, and I'm now officially a fifth grader—life doesn't get much better.

But then something happened to me today that made life worse. Way worse.

It started off well enough. Waking up when I wanted sure beat getting up at 6:00 a.m. for school. My plan after breakfast was to hit Anthony's pool today. It was scheduled to open today for the summer and it's my favorite place to go. There's a big pool with a diving board and an arcade with pinball machines. Last year the owners said they'd be getting new games for this season and I couldn't wait to try them out. On the other side of the pool, across from the arcade, is a pavilion with a digital jukebox programmed with the latest music. A lot of the kids hang out there to play card games and have a good time, so that's where I wanted be on Day One of summer vacation. I was even okay suffering with the red bathing suit

Ma bought me last week. It's so bright it practically screams, "Hey, everybody! Look at me!" The last thing I want to do is draw a lot of attention to me with my shirt off. But Ma thought I'd look great in it, so I'm stuck with it.

I was hoping Mary Lou would be there today. I met her during the last few days of the school year and she told me that she likes to go to Anthony's, too. I like her.

It's a long walk to Anthony's pool from our house. I have to go half way across town and climb Maple Street to get there, but it's worth it knowing I'm going to have a fun time. Usually I'm pretty tired just getting there. Maybe if I weren't so fat it would be easier, but I can't help it. I just like to eat and Ma's the best cook in town. I don't know why my brothers aren't fat. We all eat the same thing. I guess it's just because I'm different.

Things started out perfect. When I arrived I noticed the new pinball machines and took out my roll of quarters and started to play. After a while I decided to jump in the pool to cool off. But the thing is, I didn't want to take my shirt off. Most of the kids there don't look like me. My belly hangs over my trunks and I'm chubbier than them. But today was the first day of summer and I wanted to have a good time and there's no having a good time when you have a wet shirt flapping all around you in the water. So, off with my shirt. I was also determined not to let the way I look stop me from talking to Mary Lou—if she showed up.

I changed into the bright red trunks and locked up my shirt. As I walked out of the dressing room, I noticed Vinnie, one of the kids from my neighborhood, appear with a bunch of his buddies. He's a seventh grader and he plays on the Southwool community football team and all the girls really like him. He's so lucky. I wish that I could look like him. Maybe if Dad would buy me a set of weights like I want then I could work out. I could turn all this fat into muscle. I keep asking but he keeps saying, "No."

I watched Vinnie and his buddies walk over to the pavilion. I'm glad I didn't bump into him. He can be pretty mean. I've seen him pick on some of the kids at school just to get a laugh. All his buddies stand around as he makes fun of the kid he's picking on. He's really tough and no one fools around with him.

I jumped in the pool and enjoyed playing in the water. I love to swim, dive, and just sit and cool off. It was such a perfect summer day. The sky was crystal blue and clear—not a cloud in sight—and I was happy. I love Anthony's pool. I love any pool. If I could, I'd be a fish. Especially after what happened next.

As I got out of the water I saw Mary Lou at the concession stand. How could I get to the lockers to put on my shirt? I knew she would like me more with a shirt on than with my pudgy belly showing. I had to hang back until she walked away and then I booked it into the lockers to get my shirt. There I rehearsed my next lines over and over again. What if I said something stupid? What if she laughed at me? What if she looked at me like I was the most annoying insect on the whole planet? I kept on telling myself I can do it, I can do it, but I was really scared. I swallowed and sucked in my gut and walked over to her at the picnic table with her friends—where I completely forgot everything I'd planned to say! So, I just said hello.

Mary Lou said "Hi" back. I couldn't believe it. Wow! <u>She</u> was talking to <u>me</u>. Me. Stand back, Brad Pitt, Joe is in the HOUSE! She invited me to go to the pavilion with her and her friends to listen to music. Is this what a puppy on a leash feels like? I would follow her anywhere.

As we arrived, I noticed Vinnie inside with his buddies, hanging around and playing cards. They were smoking cigarettes. Vinnie turned and looked at me—and his face wasn't saying, "Let's be friends." My brain went into red alert. I almost spun right around and beelined out of there, but there was Mary Lou and all her friends. All of a sudden I couldn't stop thinking about the bottom of my shirt being wet from my bathing suit, outlining my stomach. I tried to pull it away so nobody would see.

I kept my head facing straight forward. As the girls and I arrived at the jukebox, Vinnie yelled, "Hey, Tubbie, looks like you got all the girls." I felt my face turn as red as my trunks. Why did he have to ruin the moment? Then he and his buddies got up and came over to the jukebox. "Hey, Tubbie, I'm talking to you," he said. "What's the matter? You don't want to talk?"

Time stopped. I was so scared, I didn't turn around until he put his hand on my shoulder and pushed me around. "I'm talkin' to you, Fatso. You got a problem with me?"

Then, brilliant me, I squeaked out, "Just leave me alone." Yeah, like that was going to stop him. His friends and some of the girls started laughing. It was so embarrassing, especially with Mary Lou standing right there.

Of course, he didn't leave me alone. Vinnie continued to make fun of me, calling me Tubbie and Fatso. And me, I just stood there frozen like some drippy red Popsicle. Finally he said, "I know your name is Yubbie. Tubbie Yubbie with a big jelly belly," and the whole planet burst out laughing and I thought I would die then and there.

Why was he doing this? How could I get away? The kids around us laughed, and he and his buddies chanted, "Yubbie, Yubbie, with a big jelly belly!" even louder. So what did I do? I bolted for the lockers, that's what I did. Big brave me. Mary Lou stayed with her friends near the jukebox, and from the doorway I swear they looked like they were flirting with Vinnie and his buddies. I didn't cry in there, but I was close.

It's a long walk from Anthony's to my house, and I cried almost the whole way. I'm still trying to figure out why Vinnie picked on me and why nobody stood up for me? I didn't do anything and I was minding my own business. Man, I looked like a total wimp! And worse, my chances with Mary Lou are probably in the toilet now. Girls don't like fat wimps.

What with being a big blubbery baby and all, I snuck into my house so my ma wouldn't see me. Up in my room I laid on my bed staring at the ceiling until I fell asleep.

At supper Ma asked me why my eyes were so red. I couldn't tell her in front of my brothers. They would've laughed at me, too. I said it was from all the swimming. Chlorine and all that stuff. She bought it. I know I should probably say something to her when we are alone, but that rarely happens. And who knows what she would say? I certainly can't tell my dad. He would think I'm a baby for being so sensitive. Even when he cracked his head on the doorway that one time, he didn't cry. He cussed up a storm and kicked a chip out of the door jam with his heavy work boot, but he didn't cry.

What do I do?

So here I am, getting ready to go to bed and writing in my journal. I hope tomorrow brings a better day. I don't even know if I can go back to Anthony's. I hate being picked on. And I really, really hate being called Yubbie. What are the odds that I'll be lucky and all the kids will forget the new nickname? Probably the same as my chances with Mary Lou: toilet city. I suppose next time when I get out of the pool I could just go and change into my shorts with a dry shirt. At least that way my stomach won't stand out. Or maybe I'll stay away from Anthony's pool for a couple of days and let things cool down. I think I'll go see Uncle Ozzie tomorrow and help him in his garden. At least he calls me Joe and appreciates my help.

Journal Entry 2 - June 24

Today was a much better day. I missed going to Anthony's, but at least I didn't get embarrassed in front of other kids. I wonder if Mary Lou thinks of me. I want to believe she's at least my friend, but after what happened yesterday she might never pay attention to me again.

It's funny how easy it is to get one over on Ma. She asked this morning if I was going to the pool and I just told her that I bumped into Uncle Ozzie yesterday and he needed some help in his garden. I can't tell her what happened, she wouldn't understand. She has her own problems to deal with. She's way sensitive and is always crying about her past. I think the fact that she was adopted and nobody ever told her the truth about her real parents upsets her. What am I but one more problem for her? Anyways, it's hard to talk about how kids pick on me—it's embarrassing—and if my brothers find out, they'll start doing the same. There's no way I can win.

Randy, my older brother by two years, would never stick up for me. He hardly even pays any attention to me because he's older and cooler. He has lots of friends, and he avoids sharing them like he does his cookies. Randy is always getting the breaks from Ma and Dad because he's their favorite. Heck, if I told him I was being picked on he'd probably slap me in the head and tell me to get a life. He doesn't have any time for my problems.

My younger brother, Trevor, would just go and start calling me the same name. For a third grader he's one mean little cuss. I have no intention of being beat up anymore at home than I am now. It's tough being the middle kid. I'm like the black sheep that nobody wants. Randy gets Dad's attention and Trevor gets Ma's. I get the cat.

At least the cat loves me.

Uncle Ozzie is a great guy. I love to work in his garden. It's fun to work on his plants and watch them grow. They need a lot of attention and care. I think sometimes that I'm their dad and I'm helping them grow strong and healthy. Eventually they will have fruit, which Uncle Ozzie tells me is the result of all the care they receive. I wonder if my ma and dad think about me that way. I need help but I'm afraid to ask. I wish they'd just treat me like a plant.

Everyone seems to be only interested in themselves. No one takes the time to ask me how I am—unless I'm puking or dying or something. But then it's only because they have to. Even Uncle Ozzie doesn't ask me how I feel about things. He's a lot like my dad. But at least he spends time with me and I can help him out.

While I was weeding I thought a lot about what happened at the pool. Yubbie is an awful name. I thought that being called Joey by Ma when she introduces me to people was bad enough. I keep telling her not to use Joey—it sounds so babyish. Totally embarrassing. But now Yubbie? How could Vinnie ever have come up with that name? I don't understand. What is so wrong with me? Just because I look different? It's not right. There I am, actually talking to a girl and starting to have a life, and then in a nanosecond the trash spills out of this guy's mouth and I'm screwed forever. Man, I wish I could have smacked him right between the eyes! Who does he think he is? Just because he's a football star he can dump his junk on everyone else? It sucks!

I was thinking this and stabbing at the weeds when Uncle Ozzie grabbed my hand and told me to go easy on his poor plants. All I could say was sorry. He'd never get it. Grown-ups never do. The sad part is that the other kids will follow Vinnie's lead now. They'll all jump in and enjoy what's happening, same as always. None of them seem to understand how bad they make me feel. It sucks being worthless and useless, and I don't need them rubbing my nose in it. It really, really hurts.

You know what? I'm going to show them all one day. I'm going to be someone. Maybe a famous star or actor, or maybe I'll become a soldier and make the rank of General. Everyone will respect me then. I'll actually be someone important. I'll have power that people will admire and then I'll treat them with disrespect and I'll show them how it feels to be picked on. They'll have to polish my medals and press my clothes and salute me. That'll show them! I'll be someone and they'll be nothing. My day will come. They'll see. I'm going to be famous and powerful and Vinnie will be nothing but dirt. And if Mr. Dirt says one word to me, I'll have him shot or put in the brig.

I keep hoping that maybe when I grow up I'll be taller and all this fat will go away. Randy is tall and he was never fat. Trevor is short with no signs of being chunky. I wish I could understand why I look this way and why I can't just be like all the rest of the kids. I don't get any answer from Ma. She just says it's okay to be chunky and that I'm healthy and growing. But she isn't the one who gets picked on.

I guess I could stop eating. I wonder how long I could stop before I would get sick, though? But then, maybe getting sick wouldn't be all that bad. Then at least someone would pay attention to me.

Journal Entry 3 - July 10

I finally got up enough courage to go back to Anthony's today. It's been over two weeks since the Vinnie thing, and I finally decided that I shouldn't have to suffer because the other kids are jerks. Plus, I just miss swimming. So I started today with a plan. I was just going to keep away from the pavilion, Mary Lou or not. It's not worth the embarrassment. I'm different and I'm just not going to fit in with those kids and that's just how it is. I would enjoy this beautiful sunny day, play some pinball and video games, and swim until my arms fall off.

For once in my life, my plan worked. I had a great day. I met two new friends at the pool. Tom, who is a tall, skinny guy with a large round head that kind of makes me think of Charlie Brown, and Danny, who is really short. You can tell Danny is smart just by the way he talks. I met them totally by accident. I jumped off the diving board like I always do and swam underwater for as long as I could hold my breath. Maybe it's my big chest or something, but I'm actually good at holding my breath. I bet I could be an Olympic swimmer—a real star—if I really wanted to. Anyways, when I finally came up I was between Tom and Danny. They were a little surprised when I popped up out of nowhere.

I apologized for almost bumping into them. Tom said it was okay and that he was impressed that I could hold my breath for such a long time. He said that maybe I should become a scuba diver for the Navy. Wow! I hadn't thought of that. He was really nice. Both Tom and Danny talked to me. It felt so good to meet new friends. They're both in fifth grade like me, but they go to the other public school in town, so I've never seen them before. They said they come to Anthony's a lot. They were better than me on the pinball machines, but I don't care because they were really cool about it. Tom's mom gave him some extra money today, so he bought us all sodas.

Then we went back to the pool, where they wanted me to teach them to hold their breath as long as I do. It takes a lot of practice, but I told them they could do it if they try hard. As I was getting out of the water I spotted Vinnie and his crew walking towards the pavilion. But they didn't notice me, thank goodness. Unfortunately, I also saw Mary Lou. She was at a table near the pavilion with her friends, not looking my way at all. She probably hasn't given me a second thought. But who cares? I had my new friends and I was going to have a good time.

Eventually Tom and Danny had to go home and so I decided to leave, too. Things worked out great. Nobody bothered us. Of course, I never had a chance to talk to Mary Lou. Someday maybe she will like me.

Tom's mom picked him up and Danny walked with me part of the way home. Danny is cool and smart! He talked about a lot of things. He loves to read and has tons of information about so many things. He likes to read books about nature, exploring, and collecting coins. I never heard about collecting coins. I thought you only spent coins, but Danny told me that certain coins are very valuable. Some are made of gold and others are very old. I almost fell through the sidewalk when he told me that some coins could be worth thousands of dollars. We high-fived when he got to his street.

So today was a good day any way you look at it. I met some new friends who are really nice. Danny's ma and dad are taking him on a trip to Europe this summer, but he said that he would see me again at Anthony's after he gets back. Europe - my geography is pretty bad. I knew it was somewhere on the other side of the Atlantic but wasn't quite sure which countries were involved. Danny laughed. He said I should read more. He told me that everything I want to know can be found in books.

Heck, I read only what I have to in class, never mind going to the library and reading more. I do what I have to in school and that's it except for comic books. I could read those all day. No one at my house reads. They just watch TV. I always tell my parents that I have no homework and so I never have to read. Why read when you can watch the tube?

So it was an awesome day. But, the thing is, if it was so great, why do I feel lonely right now? Why am I all holed up in my room, writing in this journal, without anybody to hang out with? Dad and Randy are off somewhere looking for parts for Dad's car, and Ma and Trevor are hogging the TV with their nightly game shows. I swear, that kid is attached to her apron. Everywhere she goes, he follows right behind. He's such a suck up, always squealing on Randy and me. You can't get away with anything 'cause Trevor will go running to Ma to say Joe did this and Joe did that. I wish I had a different life.

The last thing I wanted to do was look at greasy car stuff or watch annoying game shows, so I came up here to write in my journal. I feel good when I put my feelings into this book. It's like an escape. It's my world and I can make it be anything I want. I am free. I can tell anyone anything I want and they can't say anything back. I have to hide this journal real good, though, 'cause Trevor is always poking around my things, trying to take them. Of course, when I yell at him for touching my stuff, he tells Ma that I'm picking on him and I get busted.

At least when I write in my journal I can imagine my world exactly as I want it to be. Like, someday I'm going to be rich and be called "Mr. Goodman." I'll have servants and a mansion. And two flat screen TVs, a couple of Game Boys, and all the toys I want—and I won't have to share them with anyone. I'll have <u>tons</u> of money. I'll buy Mary Lou a yacht and we'll sail the open seas and go to all those places that Danny talks about. Maybe he can even be my guide. I'll pay him to be the captain of the ship and he'll take us wherever we want. I can't wait—it'll be great. Maybe I'll win the lottery or some rich relative will kick it and leave me a bunch of money.

I think I'll go back to Anthony's tomorrow and check it out. Maybe Vinnie won't show up and I can finally get a chance to talk to Mary Lou. I know if she spent some time with me we could be good friends. Or something even better. I'll wear my favorite t-shirt and use my old bathing suit that doesn't make everyone within ten miles look my way. Tom and Danny won't be there. Maybe there's a chance that Vinnie won't be there, either.

Journal Entry 4 - July 23

If there was a hole I could crawl into, I would. If there was a place I could escape to, I would fly away right this very second. If I could disappear, I'd do it, no questions asked. Why? Because this life totally bites.

It was a disaster at Anthony's today. It started off good with no Vinnie in sight as I came out of the water and saw Mary Lou next to the diving board. I sucked in my stomach and went to talk to her. She actually smiled when I said hi, like maybe she didn't think I was a total loser. So there I was, standing with my back to the pool talking to her, when all of a sudden Vinnie appears out of nowhere with his buddies. They started coming toward me. I swallowed hard and didn't know what to do.

"What are you doing talking to her, Yubbie?" Vinnie said. I swear, I can hear his mean voice in my head right now. He shook his head all sad at Mary Lou. "You don't want to hang around him, do ya? Heck, you can't even put your arms around his belly, he's so fat." At that moment, Mary Lou's friends arrived with the rest of Vinnie's buddies. This was going downhill fast. I could have tried to punch him in the face, I guess, but then he would have beat me up worse than the licking I get from Dad with the strap. I figured Mary Lou was as good as dead to me then. No way she'd give me a third chance.

But then Mary Lou surprised me, telling Vinnie to leave me alone, that we were just talking. That's when Vinnie did it. Before I could even register his arm moving, he reached out and shoved me in the chest. I went flying backwards into the pool. And of course I swallowed a ton of water. Some fish I am. As I came up coughing, I found everyone laughing. Vinnie grinned and waved then turned around and left with his buddies. I was stuck there treading water while Mary Lou looked from me to her girl friends and then finally decided to leave with them. I swear, I could kill Vinnie.

I swam back to the steps and got out of the pool. I wanted to run right over and jump on Vinnie's back and take my chances, but then I remembered Dad's words and the same thing my brother Randy says: "It takes more of a man to walk away than it does to fight." They might be right, but they are not the ones getting beat up. I feel like a big chicken because I'm afraid of hitting Vinnie. Actually, I'm not afraid to hit him, I'm afraid of what he'll do back—bash in my face. I hate feeling like a chicken. Oh, how I wish it were different. I need to do something, but I don't know what. How do I stop this torture?!!!

I hurried my way out of the pool area and walked home. All I could think about on my way was how to get Vinnie to stop. Maybe I could get a rock and hit Vinnie on his head, or maybe a stick would be better and I'd beat him until he can't get up. I want to hurt him so bad. I'm boiling mad and I can't do anything about it. I would feel so much better if I could just give him a taste of the pain I feel. Mean thoughts just kept running through my head as tears came down my face. I hate Vinnie and I hate myself.

This time when I got home, I forgot to sneak. Ma was in the kitchen. She asked me why my arm was bleeding. I didn't even know it was. I guess when Vinnie pushed me into the water, my arm hit the concrete wall of the pool and got scratched. I told her I slipped and fell near the pool and got hurt. She asked if I had been crying. I admitted to her that I was really having a bad day. She asked me what happened. She actually stopped cleaning the dishes and looked right at me, like I existed or something. I couldn't help it—I broke down and told her how Vinnie had pushed me into the pool after humiliating me in front of the other kids. I also told her that Vinnie was calling me "Yubbie." Big mistake—Trevor was standing in the doorway as I told my story, and he heard every word of it.

Ma told me not to let it bother me. Yubbie is only a name, she said, and names can't hurt me. I knew she wouldn't understand! Then she went on to tell me that if Vinnie touches me again, to let her know and she will call his parents. And before she even finished talking she was back to scrubbing some stupid pot. She wanted supper ready before my dad came home and was running really late. "Go upstairs and wash up," she told me. As if I could wash away this stupid day.

The scratches on my arm weren't too bad. They just burned a lot. As I was leaving the kitchen Trevor popped up in the hallway and said, "Hey, Yubbie. I like your new name. It fits you." I told him if he called me that name again I'd smack him in the head. He immediately yelled out, "Ma, Yubbie is going to hit me!" My ma responded by telling both of us to cut it out and get ready for supper. She didn't say anything about him calling me Yubbie. Swell. Now I'll have to listen to my new name at home—I know Trevor won't stop. I should have kept my mouth shut. What did I accomplish? Nobody really cares what I feel. Sure, Ma probably would call Vinnie's parents if I told her he picked on me again, but then what would happen? Vinnie would get mad and he'd probably beat me up next time he sees for squealing, that's what. The only thing worse than a chicken is a rat.

No one said anything about the pool thing at supper. We all stay pretty quiet when Dad gets home. He works hard, Ma tells us, and he deserves to have peace and quiet in his house. He pays the bills to support us and we have to learn to give him respect. Ma talks about all her friends and the stuff they talk about over the phone all day. Dad listens and just goes "yup" while he stuffs his face. I don't even think he cares about what Ma is telling him. He never says anything back and lets her rattle on with her gossip. My brothers and I figured out a long time ago that it's better to just eat and then take off. If we upset Dad at supper we'll pay later. Big time. So after we finished eating tonight, I went outside to take a walk. Unfortunately, so did Trevor, who whispered Yubbie as we walked out the door. I wasn't about to say anything because Dad was just on the other side. Once we got away from the house, though, I asked him to leave me alone and not to call me Yubbie. Trevor said, "You big baby. What, can't take a name?" I threatened to pound him. He immediately responded, "I'll tell Ma." Trevor is such a pain.

I took off down the street to walk around town. There's a busy street corner where the popular kids like to hang out. Thinking maybe Vinnie and his buddies might be hanging out there, I turned in the opposite direction and just kept walking. Walking lets me think. Maybe I could walk up to Mary Lou's house? It would be a major hike since she lives on Hoosac Street, one of the steepest streets in town. No, I couldn't do that. It would take me too long. I needed to be back by 8:00 p.m.

As I walked around I thought of what my perfect world would be if I had my say so: I love to swim and can swim way far while holding my breath. In my mind I see myself as an Olympic swimmer in front of a huge crowd at the end of a tournament. I've beaten every swimmer but one. I stand next to the springboard, my body all cut and toned. Muscles bulge out from my traps and shoulders. I stand super confident, waiting for the next finalist to challenge my record. And then I spot him. Coming out from the corner locker, someone is looking at me with a bit of confusion. It's Vinnie. He doesn't recognize me at first. I am a champion. When he reaches the springboard next to me I look at him and say softly, "Remember me? Yubbie? Get ready to lose."

As we each step up onto our springboard, he looks at me kind of afraid. He knows there's more than just a match at stake.

We wait for the sound of the starter gun and keep our focus on the pool. I sense him looking over, amazed that I am a winning athlete.

The gun goes off and we dive into the water. I feel a flow of energy swamp my body. I know what has to be done. As we approach the first turn around, I sense he's a little behind me and I decide to let loose. It's the last race of the day and I give it every ounce of energy I have to humiliate him. Like a dolphin putting on the after burners, my body surges like never before. I feel no resistance as I push through the water with my arms and kick with my legs. It seems the harder and faster I push, the easier it becomes. Approaching the final seconds of the race, my mind goes back to the days at Anthony's pool and the pain Vinnie caused me. Like my long walk home that long-ago day, it seems like time stood still as I touched the wall. I look at the timekeeper's clock on the wall and see that I set a new world record. I beat Vinnie by more than a minute.

Cheers and clapping explode over the stadium. I throw my hands up in the air like a victorious Olympian. Vinnie touches the wall and stands up, anxiously looking at the timekeeper's clock on the pool wall. His face goes blank when he sees how I did. He turns and looks at me and says, "Who would've believed you could become a winner?" He jumps out of the pool, puts his head down, and walks to the lockers.

I jump out of the pool as the crowd gives me a standing ovation. I wave and throw kisses, thanking them for being my fans. I see my parents and my brothers smiling in amazement. What a feeling. I did it! I became somebody important.

All of a sudden I was at the back door of my house and my dad was standing there, looking puzzled. He asked me what I was doing. I'd been standing there for a few minutes waving my hands in the air. I told him I was just swatting away a mosquito that was trying to bite me. I'm not sure he accepted my explanation. But hey, I had to think quickly, and that's all I had at the time.

I ran up stairs to write this entry into my journal. I know someday that I will become somebody important. Everyone will stop making fun of me and I will not be a joke. I'm going to bed now and am going to try to dream about the swim story. I can't wait to see me receiving the gold medal.

Journal Entry 5 - August 1

Wow! I was really excited today to get a call from Tom, that guy I met at Anthony's pool the other day. He asked me if I wanted to go to Renfruit Field and play some baseball with his friends. They needed an extra body and he thought of me. He's a good guy.

I had to be honest with him. I told him that I'm not much of a baseball player. I have a glove, but I don't get out and play often. Well, it's mostly the truth. I couldn't really tell him that no one around here wants me to play on their team because I'm so bad. I really want to be good, but it doesn't come easy.

So I waited for Tom to hang up on me when I said that but he didn't. He told me not to worry about it. "We're just a bunch of kids getting together to have fun." So I decided to go. Mistake!

When I got to the field Tom introduced me to his friends. They were really nice. We chose teams and started to play. They asked me what position I wanted to play. Knowing how bad I play, I told them I would play right field. I figured that was the best position because normally everyone hits it to center or left field. I thought I'd be safe.

I was right. During the first inning, not so much as a pop fly in right field. I walked into the dugout relieved. Everyone decided the batting order, and I kinda sat back and waited until everyone chose a spot. I was happy that I was the last batter up. It might even take a couple of innings before I had to get up and prove myself.

We were having a great time. I was yelling, cheering my

teammates on, telling them that they could do it, that they could smack it out over the fence. What a team we had. We were doing great. After a couple of innings we were ahead.

My turn up to bat. The bases were loaded and we had two outs. I remembered Tom's words as I left the dugout. "You can do it, Joe, it's up to you. Hit a grand slam. Wale it out of the park."

Talk about freaking out. As I walked up to the plate I thought of how I should have told Tom this morning how bad I really am. Everyone was relying on a kid who couldn't hit a barn with a boulder, never mind hit this small ball with a stick.

First pitch—first strike. I looked down the field at my teammates on the bases cheering me on. Second pitch—ball. Phew! Third pitch—strike two. I started to sweat and I could feel my knees shaking. I needed to hit the ball. Everyone was counting on me and I couldn't let them down. I brought my bat back so I could hit the ball as hard as I could. The pitcher wound up and released the pitch. I could see the ball coming and released every ounce of energy I had—and missed. Strike three!

The inning was over but we were still ahead. Tom wasn't upset. He said, "No problem, Joe. Tough break. You'll get it next time." No one was upset at me as the other players ran into the dugout. I was shocked. I had just screwed up and nobody said a thing.

The game went on. It was the top of the ninth, the score was tied, and not a single ball had entered my side of the outfield all game. The opposing team had one left-hand hitter. He had grounded out a couple of times and hit a few base hits. He was up.

I stood in the outfield, focused on his every swing. He had one strike and three balls. Then it happened. The lefty hit a pop fly into right field. I kept my eyes on the ball as it flew through the air. I ran as hard as I could but I swear my legs wouldn't move as fast as I needed. My heart was pounding and I charged forward.

I could see it coming down. I was close but out of breath and pushed so hard with my legs that I tripped and fell to the ground. Nightmare! I rolled a few feet but somehow still managed to get up and run to the ball. It had landed nearby. I picked it up and tried to blast it to the second baseman—but my throw was a bit off and kinda went toward the third baseman instead. They scored two runs because of me. Shoot. Has anyone ever dug a hole in right field and buried himself during a game?

The inning was over and we went back to the dugout. I didn't know what to say to the guys so I just said, "I'm sorry." I went over to Tom and said, "I told ya I'm not really a good player." "It's okay," he said. But I could tell he was disappointed. There was silence in the dugout.

It was the bottom of the ninth. My team was able to get the score up again and we were only one run behind. I felt good. We had a chance. The next batter struck out and I found myself up to bat again. Man, I hated being in that position. Two outs, with a man on first and third and Clumsy up to bat. Why me? It's bad enough to strike out during an inning, but to be the end of the game with it all on my shoulders was too much.

I stood in the batter's box telling myself, Calm down, relax, take your time, you can do it. The first ball came blasting toward me and I swung. Strike! I kept repeating, "Joe, you can do it. Relax. Take your time." I watched the pitcher wind up and release the ball. CRACK! I hit it! I was so shocked I just stood there like a doofus and watched the ball head down the first baseline. Unfortunately, the ball went out of bounds. Now I had <u>two</u> strikes and no balls. I was really nervous.

I looked around and could see the excitement in the field rising. My team was yelling, "You can do it! You can do it!" The other team's players were yelling, "You're gonna choke! You're gonna choke!" The pitcher let the ball go, and things seemed to slow down. I don't even remember swinging, but I'll never forget what I heard. "Strike three! You're out!"

I dropped the bat and walked off the field—all the way off. Straight toward the street and everything. Why bother staying? I'd let them down. What a screw up! All kind of thoughts went through my head all the way home, and I hated every one of them. Why can't I do anything right? I should have told Tom "no" when he invited me to play. At least then I would still have a friend. Now I'm just the loser who lost the game and he'll probably never talk to me again.

So here I am again, laying in bed writing in this stupid journal. Like it does any good. I don't even know why I keep writing. It's a waste of time. My whole life is a waste of time. I'm clumsy, fat, and uncoordinated. I suck at everything! No wonder I don't have many friends.

Maybe someday it will change. If I lose all my weight and join the baseball team, maybe the coach can teach me how to play. It's not like Dad would teach me. He isn't interested in sports. He only likes to take things apart and put them back together. And he only has time for his pet, Randy, anyway. And Ma just likes cooking or crying in the phone or whatever. And Trevor—aw, who cares what Trevor likes? All I know is that there's no one in this house who can help me out. If I had a coach, then I could become someone.

Maybe I could become another Babe Ruth, even. I can see it now. Just like it happened today, it would be the last inning. Two outs, the score tied, and guess who's up to bat? Me—the second Babe Ruth. The crowd is going ballistic, screaming and waving their hands and everything. I walk up to the plate like I own it. I decide to put the ball right out the left side of the park. I can see the ball leave the park in my mind, like it was propelled by a rocket launcher. No problem, I tell myself. It's outta here, no problem.

First ball—strike. I look at the ump with a scowl. Doesn't he know a ball when he sees it? But I stay focused. I give the pitcher a stare, challenging him to send his best. I grasp the bat and swagger it back and forth, feeling its power. It wants to explode, I can feel it. I stop for a second, letting the bat touch the plate and pointing to the left side of the field. The crowd stands, cheering me on. I've shown them where I aim to hit it, but they don't know if I really can. Silly mortals! Of course I can. The cheers get so loud that the announcer's voice fades into the background.

I bring the bat back over my shoulder, waving it in the air. The pitcher winds up and flings the fastest pitch ever clocked. My focus is so great that the ball seems to slow down, positioning itself to be hit. I release the bat with the force of an atom bomb—a loud crack shatters the crowd's cheers. Just like I promised, the ball flies high into left field. The roar of the crowd is deafening as the ball goes right out of the park. We win!

As I leave the baseball stadium, thousands of people line up to get my autograph. What a rush! I'm the hero of the day.

Journal Entry 6 - August 12

Well, only two more weeks and back to school. Not soon enough for me after today.

I went to Anthony's after an unexpected call from Tom the other day. I couldn't believe it: He asked me if I wanted to play some more baseball. Yeah, and I want to sing the national anthem at the World Series. Was he crazy?! I had to make up an excuse. I told him I had a lot of things to do with my ma and I couldn't get out of it. There was no way I was going to set myself up for embarrassment and failure again.

Tom told me everyone wondered what happened to me the day we played. They looked around after the game and I was gone. He told me they all went to Ocharski's for a soda and wanted me to join in. Wow, that was really nice of them, especially after I let them down. Now I felt like a double loser, running away like that and all. I told him the reason I left was because I had to hurry home since my dad was coming home early and taking us out to McDonald's for supper. I couldn't tell him the truth.

Tom told me that Danny was back from Europe and they were going up to Anthony's for the day and invited me along. I was happy that he still wanted to be my friend. I couldn't believe it!

It was a beautiful sunny day, and I met Tom on the way up to Maple Street. We talked a lot on the way. He's a very interesting guy. He likes sports and plays them at his school. Because he's tall he likes basketball, but he's also a pitcher on his baseball team. We talked a little about what happened at the game. I told him I was sorry I let the team down. I was shocked at his reaction. "Joe, it's only a game. You gave it your best and that's all anyone expects of you. Most of us play on a team in the town's baseball league so we practice a lot. When we play in the summer, it's for fun."

He made me feel good, relieved that even though I blew it, the kids didn't hate me for it.

Danny met us at the entrance and he started telling us about his trip and all the foreign countries he had seen with his parents. They went to England, France, Germany, and more. He talked about all the interesting things they saw, like the Eiffel Tower, Buckingham Palace where the Queen lives, and the high mountains called the Alps. He's so smart. It's hard for me to believe he can get that much information into his head. Just listening about it made my head hurt after awhile. Heck, I can't even remember everything he said.

We played pinball and video games and went swimming. Then Vinnie showed up. We were inside the main building playing a game when he and his buddies walked in. I wanted to bust out of there, but I was with Tom and Danny, and I didn't want them to see me running away again. Plus, I figured Vinnie wouldn't mess with me with them there. Still, I kept one eye on him as he approached the machines. So much for not messing with me in front of Tom and Danny: As he walked by, Vinnie dropped his shoulder and bumped right into me with such a jerk that it made the machine tilt.

"Excuse me, Yubbie," he said, looking all surprised. "I think your belly got in the way and you tilted your machine. Too bad, Fatso." And then he and his flunkies laughed and kept walking toward the lockers.

Tom and Danny looked at me and Danny asked, "What was up with that jerk? And why did he call you Yubbie?" Does it get more embarrassing? I didn't answer them at first but then Danny kept asking and finally I told them that Vinnie had been picking on me all summer and that he'd made up that name one day at the pavilion.

Danny said, "Don't pay attention to that jerk. What the heck does he know, anyway? He might be good at football, but he doesn't have an ounce of brains. My dad says that kids like him have the problem, not us. Something is definitely wrong with him."

Tom added, "We have a guy just like Vinnie at our school who picks on all the kids. He'll get his someday. Just wait and see. Don't pay attention to him and he'll go back to his cave."

It made me feel a little better to hear them say those things. But Vinnie wasn't picking on them. I wondered what they'd do if they were in my shoes.

Danny put another quarter in the machine and turned to me and said, "Here you go, Joe. It's on me." That was cool of him.

I wasn't half way through the song when I saw Vinnie and his buddies coming back from the locker room dressed in bathing suits. As he passed I tensed, my body getting ready for another blow. Instead he bent over and whispered in my ear, "See you outside later, Yubbie," and walked out the door. I noticed that the owner was looking our way. Maybe he saw what happened before and was keeping an eye on Vinnie? Yeah, that's probably why Vinnie didn't do anything. It wasn't that he suddenly turned into a great guy in that locker room.

The rest of the day went okay. We stayed away from Vinnie when we went swimming and I thought it might be over for the day. Late afternoon we got out of the water and decided to change. Tom and Danny had to get going because Danny's mother was picking them up. They offered me a ride home. As much as I liked the idea, I turned them down, telling them I had to stop downtown on my way to pick something up. The thing is, I'd seen Mary Lou earlier during the day and I wanted to say hi to her. Vinnie was nowhere in sight, so I might actually have a chance to talk with her.

I was coming out of the main building heading in her direction when all of a sudden I was grabbed by the shirt and pulled around the corner. It was that stupid jerk, Vinnie! He tossed me into the wall and said, "I told you I would see you later. Who are your new friends? Meat Head and Squirrelly? You guys look like the Three Musketeers. Or should I call you MOUSEketeers? One tall, one short, and of course there's you, Fatso. Three rats in a pack."

I was so scared I couldn't catch my breath. Pinned to the wall, I couldn't move. Sweat poured down my face. My voice was quivering like a total wimp but at least I finally got out the words: "Leave them alone. They're nice guys."

"Oh, don't worry about them. Worry about what I'm going to do to you."

Why was he doing this to me? I hadn't done anything to him. Why couldn't he just leave me alone? I couldn't believe it. Maybe Tom and Danny were right, maybe Vinnie was the one with the problem and not me. Only, stupid me, I said all that out loud.

Vinnie's face turned bright red and he shoved his ugly mug

right up in my face. Our noses were almost touching. "Why? I'll tell you why. Because I don't like you, Fatso," he said. "Yubbie is a slob. Yubbie is fat, ugly, and gutless. That's why."

He told me I'd better shut my big fat mouth before he put his fist down my throat. "Then you'll have something to complain about, Fatso."

I didn't utter a word.

Then he surprised me. He said he needed cigarettes and demanded mine. I didn't understand what he meant at first. I didn't have cigarettes! When I told him that, he said he wanted money, did I have any money? "No." "Listen, Fatso," he said, getting up in my face again. "If you're lying, I'm gonna beat you within an inch of your life. I said, do you got any money?" I nodded my head meaning yes. Stupid me! "How much?" he said. I reached into my pocket and took out all my money. He grabbed it out of my hand and told me to get lost or he'd kick my butt.

My legs couldn't move fast enough. I bolted around the corner and headed home. Stupid, chicken me! That was all I'd had left of my weekly allowance. Now I'm broke and can't buy any candy until next week or go back to Anthony's because I don't have the money to pay to get in.

All the way home I just thought about how much I hated Vinnie. I know that hating is bad, but he's so mean. I just want to hurt him. Maybe when he was swimming today I could have pulled him under water and held him down until he couldn't breathe. I can hold my breath for a long time so he would drown and I would be done with him.

So that's it. I'm done for the summer. I am not going back to Anthony's again. Forget Mary Lou. Every time I want to talk to her, Vinnie appears like some evil genie out of a bottle. How does he know? If I don't go back then I won't have to deal with him again. Maybe I'll get lucky and he'll jump off the high diving board and hit his head on the concrete wall. Bang! The world would be better off.

I gotta go to bed. I'm so tired. Someday I'm going to beat Vinnie at his own game. When I get slim, I'm going to take a martial arts class and be like Bruce Lee. He's the best and the fastest. Next time Vinnie grabs my shirt, I'll grab his hand and toss him around like a sack of potatoes. I'll throw him twenty feet in the air and let him slam on the ground. And when he gets up, I'll hit him fifty times with my martial arts punches before he can even blink an eye.

And just for good measure, I'll spin around and hit him with a spin kick and send him flying through the wall. That'll teach him. Oh, and I'll take his stupid cigarettes and break them over his ugly head and then I'll take all the money out of his pockets and call <u>him</u> Fatso. As I walk away I'll tell him, "Now we're even, punk."

Journal Entry 7 - September 6

Fifth grade, middle school. Bigger kids. I thought being in fifth grade was going to be cool, but it turns out now I'm low guy on the totem pole.

Trevor didn't make the first day any better. He may go to the elementary school, but that's just across the street from my school, which means he and his buddies walk the same way I do. The whole way there, they followed me on the other side of the street yelling out my new name. I just wanted to bust over there and slap every one of them in the head. But what would that get me? He'd only go home and tell Ma I was picking on him. I can't win. So now his buddies have a new game—calling me Yubbie.

They won't be able to bother me during the day, though. Instead, the kids at my school have that covered. There I was walking down the corridor of my new school where hardly any of my classmates should know me and all of a sudden some kid from across the lockers yells out, "Hey, Yubbie, how's it goin'?" I just wanted to melt into the floor and disappear.

What was I supposed to say? I mean, the kid didn't really say anything mean or chant the Yubbie Tubbie jingle like Vinnie. This kid just called out Yubbie, like he'd heard it around at Anthony's and really thought it was my name. I hate the name, but I wasn't going to start anything the first week of middle school. At this rate I might have to get used to the name. I just said "Hi" and moved on.

Well, then I turned the corner to my homeroom and BANG! I almost knocked over Mary Lou. Wow! I was so excited to see her. I stumbled out a "Hi." Fortunately there was no Vinnie this time! He's now in seventh grade at the junior high down the street.

We talked for a minute. She told me that she looked for me a couple of times at Anthony's but either I wasn't around or I was hanging out with a couple of other kids. She must have been talking about Tom and Danny. She didn't want to barge in, she said. What, is she shy? Who would've guessed? She always seemed so sure of herself. Anyway, hearing that made me feel so good. Mary Lou likes me!

She apologized about the times Vinnie interrupted our conversations. She told me that her friends like the boys who play in the local community football league and think they're hot stuff. She's not impressed and felt that Vinnie had no right to pick on me. She didn't know what to do. She felt like she had to hang around with the girls she came with, and they wanted to hang around the football players. So that's what she did. She told me she felt bad for me.

I brushed it off. "That's okay. He really didn't bother me. He'll get his one day." Maybe she believed it. I don't know. She smiled and nodded and all.

But none of that even mattered, because what she did next still makes me want to jump up and down. She gave me her phone number. Seriously! Then she told me it would be okay if I called her at home. Wow. No, double wow, and holy macarollee!

I died and went to heaven. I could feel my blood rushing to my face and my jaw getting tight.

"Thanks. I'll give you a call," is all I managed. She smiled and walked away.

I felt like I was floating as I entered homeroom. I was so far gone that the teacher had to repeat my name twice in roll call. I couldn't get Mary Lou out of my head. She's very pretty. She may look a little different than the other girls because she's a little rounder than most, but who cares. She's totally sweet and has beautiful blue eyes that sparkle.

The rest of the day was a ton of nothing. I met a couple of guys from my class. They didn't seem so interested in getting to know me. At recess they were all playing baseball on the playground and no one asked me to join in. Just as well. I probably would've made a fool of myself, anyway, tripping over my big fat feet and dropping the ball. Not the way to start new friendships.

I sat on the swing and gazed out into the sky thinking about the phone call I was going to make later. My thoughts ran wild trying to decide on all the questions I had for Mary Lou. I really want to get to know her.

When school was out I had to deal with Trevor and his buddies and all their "Hey, Yubbie!" yelling from across the street. I tried to ignore them because I was having such a great day and looking forward to calling Mary Lou.

At home I changed and told Ma that I needed to go to the store and would be back for supper. I flew down the street to get to the nearest pay phone to call Mary Lou. Ma doesn't let us have cell phones, and no way was I calling from the house. Randy calls his girlfriend from home and takes the phone into the coat closet to have the conversation. Trevor and I know better than to bother him while he's on the phone. He'd just as soon crack it over our heads as tell us to shut up. And it's not like I could use our phone, anyway. Randy gets on it as soon as he gets home and then hogs it till suppertime. Even if I could, Trevor wouldn't let me get away with the closet trick. He'd be pounding on the door, trying to get me mad so I'd lose my temper. The pay phone sounded good to me.

I called Mary Lou's number but it was busy. I stood around for another ten or fifteen minutes, but every time I called the line was busy. I stayed waiting for an hour, and the line was busy the whole time. I felt like calling the operator and telling her it was an emergency so she would break into the line, but I didn't think Mary Lou would appreciate that.

Finally I gave up and walked down to Sierra Street and headed for the woods. The woods are very special to me. I can chill there, and my thoughts run so free. I like to go up the Tofic River as it winds through the mountains. It's so pretty. The water is crystal clear and pure. You can feel the mist from the waterfalls as you hike up the cliffs. The river looks like it was carved out by a glacier that cut through the valley or maybe like the earth split open millions of years ago leaving jagged cliffs on both sides. It probably happened in prehistoric times.

I eventually got to Indian Rock, one of the biggest boulders on the river. I stood on top of it looking down at the riverbed below. Just like a revered chief of a tribe, I could see my people below awaiting my words of great wisdom. I could see my bride, Mary Lou, near the shore, smiling and embracing me with those glittering blue eyes. I told my tribe that it was important to understand our journey. We could make the choice to go to battle as all the brave warriors desired, or we could continue up river to the land of peace and plenty.

As their leader, I told them it was a time to choose peace.

Thinking of the word "time" made me realize it was way past time to get my butt home. I'd told Ma I'd only be gone an hour. That was two hours ago! I'd spent an hour just trying to get through to Mary Lou. I started up the trail through the cliffs, taking the short cut home, walking as fast as I could.

Ma was really mad. I'd missed supper and they were freaked out that something had happened to me. I told them I was all right. But it didn't matter—Dad was even madder than Ma and had the strap out. I knew what was coming. Dad's been using that old-fashioned straight razor sharpening belt for as long as I can remember. The thing is about twelve inches long and three inches wide, and it hurts. I repeated how sorry I was and that it wouldn't happen again. Dad screamed at me and told me to go to my room without supper and that I was lucky that he didn't use his behavior corrector today on my butt. "Next time I'll give you a lickin' and you'll be grounded for a week."

Sometimes I hate my dad. When he hits me with the strap it really hurts. Ma tells us that he loves us—even though he never says it. She tells me that my dad's father disciplined him with a strap, too. I wish his dad had thought of a better way. I don't think it's right to be hit with a piece of leather. I shiver in my shoes and feel my body go numb every time he pulls that thing out. Someday it's going to disappear and we won't have to worry. Besides, Dad had no business treating a chief with such disrespect. In the old days that wouldn't be tolerated and he'd be skinned alive and roasted at the stake.

I'm hungry. But maybe not eating is a good thing—I'll lose some fat.

Journal Entry 8 - October 15

What a blast! I just came back from my first camping trip. Danny asked me a couple of weeks ago to go on a Columbus Day camping trip with his dad. Tom was going, too. I love the woods and jumped at the chance to go, so happy that Ma and Dad let me. I needed to get out of that house.

Danny's father is really cool. He's a lawyer and super smart, like Danny. The things he knows about the outdoors are amazing. The two of them are like walking encyclopedias on nature.

Best of all I got away from Trevor who has been really mean to me lately. He just won't quit. He even tried to talk Ma into making me take him on this campout. Yeah, right! No chance, no way. I told Ma that there was only room for four in the tent, so Trevor was out of luck.

You have to know how to be quick on your feet when you make up stories. People won't just accept the truth sometimes or you could get a good lickin' if you can't make up a good fib. I'm really fast with the excuses. I get away with it all the time. Well, most of the time.

The first day we had to set up the campsite. They taught me how to pitch a tent, gather wood for a campfire, put rocks in a circle to build a fire, and how to store food at night so the bears don't get at it. I nearly climbed back into the truck then and there when they said bears. But Danny's dad said that bears don't usually bother people. There are only black bears in this part of the country, and they don't eat people. He said they're just as afraid of us as we are of them but I don't know how much I believe him. I mean, the bears are the ones with big teeth and claws. My braces and stubby little fingers aren't going to make them pee their pants.

Danny's dad told us that as long as the bear can't smell food and we don't keep food in the tent, the bears won't come near the campsite. He should know, since he's been camping for a long time and has yet to come face to face with a bear. So finally I decided maybe I wouldn't be bear chow this weekend after all.

I had my first meal cooked on a campfire—hot dogs, beans, and bug juice. Well, it was really fruit juice, but that's what campers call it. We had to find sticks to use to cook the dogs. Danny's dad went in the woods with us, looking for the perfect sticks. They have to be from a live tree so they won't catch on fire from all the heat. He took out this huge knife, almost as big as Rambo's survival knife, and cut off the branches we chose. Seeing that, I felt even better about the bear thing. And I swore to sleep close to Danny's dad.

We all sat around the fire and cooked our dogs. He also built some kind of tripod thingee to hang the pot of beans from. I swear, the whole setup looked like something on an old west cattle run. The sky was clear with millions of stars sparkling in the heavens, and the smell of bacon in the beans lingered in the air. Wow! What a treat.

Of course, we had chores. Danny's dad told us that part of camping is working as a team. Everyone has to help out. "We have to rely on each other out here," he said. "We each help the others be successful." I wish we had some of that at my house.

Things are so different between Danny and his dad. Even though Danny is his son, he treated us all the same. He asked me questions about me. That was the first time any adult asked me how I felt about things. He asked me if I had a girlfriend. I told him about Mary Lou and that we were becoming friends. He asked me about school and what I liked most about it, and what kind of books I like to read. That was a hard question to answer, so I told him I like comic books and left it at that. He asked me what I wanted to be. I told him I never thought about it.

I liked how Danny's dad treated me. How they all treated me. I belonged. I was a part of something. It made me feel special. Nobody was pushing me around.

After we ate, we cleaned up and put all the food away. We didn't want any visiting animals during the night! Then, we all sat around the fire with our bug juice and Danny's dad broke out a bag of marshmallows and some chocolate bars and graham crackers. He told us we were going to make s'mores. I never heard of s'mores before, but I knew as long as they had chocolate and marshmallows, they'd be good. And they were!

We sat around the fire and Danny's dad told us about all the great things they had done and seen in Europe. I especially loved the stories about hiking in the Alps. They saw rams as big as furry cows going up sheer cliffs. That's where they live and that's what they do—they climb cliffs. He told us that when they got to the top of one mountain they could see for hundreds of miles as they overlooked mountains and valleys. I just sat there lost in his stories. Danny's so lucky to have such a great dad!

We all went to bed late. I was happy that they put me in the middle of the tent. I figured that if a bear decided to come in, he would step on someone else first. It was scary to listen to the noises of the night. There were all kinds of creatures out there making weird sounds. I told myself that no one else in the tent was afraid, so I shouldn't be either, and I fell asleep.

The next two days were filled with all kinds of exciting adventures. We walked on trails that brought us to monstrous waterfalls. They must have been a mile high or so. The water came down like the Hoover dam letting loose.

We saw all kinds of trees and plants. Danny's dad showed us poison ivy and told us never to touch this plant. If you do, you'll get blisters all over your body and itch for a week. I thought, heck, it can't be any worse than the marks that my dad leaves on my body with the strap. They burn for days.

We went swimming in ice-cold water, hiked to the top of a ridge overlooking the valley, and saw a bunch of wild turkeys feeding in the woods. I never knew what a real live turkey looked like. They don't look like the pictures we color in school or the bird that's usually on the table at Thanksgiving. I even asked if they were the same and if that's how we got Thanksgiving birds—from the woods. Danny's dad said the ones we eat are raised on farms so they can get big and fat which makes them tender and juicy. The turkeys roaming the woods are not fat and probably chewy. Does that make me juicy and tender? Maybe the bear would walk in the tent and choose me first because I'm not chewy.

The weekend was filled with a ton of adventures. It was one of the best I ever had. Not only did we do a lot of exciting things, but Tom, Danny, and his dad were interested in me and made me feel good. It was hard for me to want to come home. I wish I could have stayed out in the woods. No Trevor, no Vinnie, no Yubbie, no school, and no strap. Perfect.

The best of the best was that Danny's dad asked me if I wanted to join the Boy Scouts. He said they do this kind of stuff all the time. First I would have to turn eleven, which happens in a couple of weeks. Danny turns eleven in the spring and he plans to join. Tom just turned eleven so he can join any time. I told them that I'd have to talk to my parents, but I'd like to become a Scout. Camping is cool.

I haven't said anything to Ma and Dad yet. I did tell them I had a great time this weekend but they were kinda busy with other things so I came upstairs to write about my adventure. Maybe I'll become another Davy Crocket, king of the wild frontier. I remember my dad watching one of those oldie TV stations and I guess there was a series mega years ago on the Disney Channel about a woodsman called Davy Crocket. I remember the corny song they played at the beginning of the show. It talked about Davy Crocket as a great hunter and explorer. I guess he was born in Tennessee and it said he killed a bear when he was three.

Davy killed a bear when he was only three? Hard to believe. But I could be like him. If a bear tried to get into our tent, I would take out my huge Bowie knife and fight him. I can see it now. I'd be the hero of the day as I wrestled a gaint grizzly in the mountains of Tennessee. It sounds like they have a lot of them there. The grizzly comes out of nowhere and starts charging a family hiking in the woods. I jump off a boulder onto his back just before he gets to the three little children. The grizzly throws me off his back and slams me into a tree. I get up and shake it off. The bear is now upset with me and stands up, making roaring sounds that can be heard for miles. He drops back to all fours like thunder and sets his eys on me and charges. I hold my ground. As he nears me, he stands up again swinging his gaint paws with claws that are twelve inches long. I fall to the ground and roll away, but not before he catches me with one of his swipes and tears my sheepskin jacket. Unacceptable! I jump up and charge right back at him, stabbing him in the chest over and over. The grizzly roars in pain as my Bowie knife takes its toll. Finally, the bear begins to fall. I have to jump out of the way so it doesn't fall on me. The grizzly hits the ground so hard the woods shake and a giant thunk is heard.

I jump on its back and finish the job. When I finally get off the bear, the family surrounds me, thanking me for saving their lives. I'm the hero. I have some cuts and scrapes, but I stand strong and victorious. They tell all the newspapers and TV stations about what happened and a picture of me appears on the nightly news. Wow!

Journal Entry 9 - October 24

Who waits for birthdays? Me! I waited for this day for over a year. I'm now eleven—almost a teen. Ma asked me a couple of weeks ago if I wanted to have some friends over for my birthday. Other than Tom and Danny, I didn't know who to ask. I could have asked Mary Lou. I just told Ma that it was too close to Halloween and most kids were getting ready for the big night. She bought it.

Mary Lou and I have talked a couple of times since I finally reached her by phone. One day at school she told me what happened when I couldn't get through. She has the same problem as I do: an older sister, Cindy, who hogs the phone as much as Randy. Mary Lou is always left waiting, just like I am.

So we came up with a plan. I would contact Mary Lou around 6:00 at night, after supper. That way, she could get my calls. She's really nice. We talk about a lot of things.

I guess her sister Cindy picks on her and calls her "stupid" and "melon head." Mary Lou is a little round at the waist, but not enough to get picked on. She'll probably grow out of that and be beautiful some day. She doesn't have this big piece of fat hanging over her belt like me, like the foam of an ice cream soda overflowing the glass. She says her sister's insults make her feel rotten. She's happy that she has a bunch of girlfriends who accept her and let her hang around with them. She doesn't agree with all the things they do, but she wants to have friends.

I told her I really understood about getting picked on. Not only do I have a brother who does it, but now half of my middle school is calling me Yubbie. The name is stuck to me like a fly on flypaper and I can't get it off. I like talking to her and I know she would have come to my party if I had one. Heck, she doesn't even know it's my birthday.

I've been asking Ma for a special gift for my birthday, hoping to get my first guitar. I also want weights and a dog, but a guitar would do me for now. In the last year I've been listening to the radio a lot and thought I might want to learn to play an instrument and be a singer like Joe Jonas of the Jonas Brothers. All the girls love them. Joe Jonas has five guitars and his brother Kevin has fifteen. If I started now I could be on the stage in no time. So that's why I want a guitar.

Not that I usually get what I really want. Instead, Ma goes out and buys the gift she thinks I'd like. And what <u>she thinks</u> and what <u>I like</u> are very different. She even buys me green shirts. I hate the color green! Ma says I look good in green. Who cares?

I like to sing. When I was little, Ma taught me all the usual kiddie songs, and I'm good at Christmas carols. The girls go crazy every time the Jonas Brothers get on stage. I know I can be just like them. I could hire someone to chisel off this fat gut because I'd have all the money I'd need. I'd be rich. Everyone would want my attention. They'd scream for my autograph, and I'd have all the girls I want. Nobody would reject me or call me Yubbie.

Best of all, I wouldn't have to worry about Vinnie. I'd have my bodyguards take him to the side and chuck him in the Dumpster in the alley behind the stage.

Dad finally came home and my birthday celebration began. Ma cooked my favorite—hard-boiled eggs over toast with her special white cream sauce and butter. It's the best. We usually have it for lunch, but on our birthdays we can have any meal we want. I ate four helpings.

Ma also baked me my favorite cake—pistachio with a cream cheese frosting. She had chocolate treats surrounding the cake, and it was all mine. I had two big pieces. Everything was going right.

I sat back and felt really stuffed, happily waiting for my gift. I must have told Ma a thousand times that I wanted a guitar. I was sure there was no way she could think I wanted anything else. I even wrote it on the note board by the telephone and in the dust on top of the coffee table one day. I couldn't wait. I kept thinking maybe she'd bought me a Fender Stratocaster. Then I could become a lead guitarist. Or maybe she'd bought me an acoustic folk guitar like the one Kevin Jonas plays. If she bought me an electric guitar she'd definitely have to buy me an amp, too. I was excited and anxious as Ma went into her coat closet.

Sure enough, she pulled out this big package. Yes! It was too big for a dog and not heavy enough for weights, so it had to be a guitar. Score!

I nearly freaked out then and there, seeing a cardboard box shaped like a guitar. Trevor sat up and looked surprised. Bet he didn't think I'd get one! I ripped off the wrapping paper and opened the box. It was a guitar, all right. Only, it wasn't a Fender Stratocaster or an electric guitar. It wasn't even an acoustic folk guitar. It was an acoustic Spanish guitar like they use on the old fogey stations playing ballroom music. A big, clunky, ugly guitar. I almost fell through the floor. What was I going to say? Ma was looking at me all proud and happy. I couldn't hurt her feelings. Finally I said, "Wow! It's perfect. I really wanted a guitar." Really I wanted to puke all the rich food I just ate all over the kitchen floor. If I was lucky, I'd get some on Trevor's shoes as he laughed away.

How could she have bought me this monstrosity of a guitar? I thought I had a big belly. This thing was enormous, so big that it completely covered me from below my belly to my chest. I thought maybe she bought it to cover up my fat. Why does stuff like this always happen to me? Why?

Turns out she'd wanted to make it a surprise so she went down to the local music store and asked the owner, Mr. Coachtree, what he recommended. Why'd she do that? He's old! He had no idea about the kind of guitar I wanted. Totally ruining my whole future, he told her that this would be a good learning guitar and that once I learned, I could move up to something different.

At least he had something right. I definitely wanted to move up to something different—but right now. I'd never get on stage with this big, fat guitar. Not only would I keep the name Yubbie, but Vinnie might come up with some jerky name for my fat guitar. Holding it made me look like something out of Star Wars. Maybe Jabba the Hutt?

It's almost time to go to bed. Why does life seem so complicated? It can be so simple. If Ma would've asked me to go down to the music store with her before my birthday, I would've shown her the kinds of guitars I wanted. Then she could've chosen one of them as my gift. I know she loves me and was trying to buy me a special gift. Dad works hard and money is tight sometimes, but it wasn't about how much the guitar cost, it was about the type I wanted.

They told me that I could take lessons from the old guy who sold her the guitar. Swell—he'll probably have me learning something from World War II. I don't want to take lessons from him. What I do want is to walk into his store then trip and fall on the guitar, smashing it into a zillion pieces. With my luck, though, Trevor would see and rat me out.

Well, I wanted a guitar and I got what I wanted so maybe I should be happy and thankful at that. I'll have to get used to it, I guess, like I'm getting used to being called Yubbie. It hurts at first, but it gets easier in time. Maybe the lessons won't be so bad.

Up in my room with the guitar right next to me, I can see it all now. Kevin Jonas is on stage introducing their special guest singer and guitarist: Joe Striker. Isn't that the coolest stage name ever? I walk up on stage looking all lean and cool. I've got on a leather jacket and t-shirt —no belly to hide whatsoever—and I plug in my guitar. I rip out a tune that gets the whole audience screaming. Everyone loves me. My voice hits impossible notes. Even the Jonas Brothers look at me in amazement. I'm the star of the night as the audience keeps cheering me on for more.

I throw out kisses to all the girls and raise my hands. "Thank you!" I yell. "Thanks to the best fans ever!" They cheer so loud I'll have to shout out my next song. It'll be the best concert ever.

Journal Entry 10 - December 21

It's the worst day ever. The stupid tears won't stop dripping onto my journal. I can't see very clearly and I'm shaking so hard I can barely write. But I have to write about what happened, because what else can I do? Maybe I should just jump out the window and my problems will be gone.

It started on the way home from school today. It was overall a pretty good day. I'm getting pretty used to being called Yubbie. Most kids don't make fun of me. They just think Yubbie is my name. I guess that's okay.

It was cold on the way home. It snowed six inches a couple of days ago and the temperature has fallen into the teens. The wind was making my cheeks sting. Ma bought the three of us new boots, coats, scarves, gloves, and hats. New England winter can be pretty brutal, so she makes sure we dress for the bad weather.

I was walking home, minding my own business, when I spotted Vinnie and his buddies coming down the street. I didn't have time enough to bolt down one of the side alleys before he saw me. He waved to his buddies to start running toward me. I could hear him say, "Let's go talk to Yubbie."

In seconds they were all around me. Vinnie started by saying, "Hey, Yubbie, nice hat. I'm surprised they make hats for walrus heads like you. Did Mommy knit little porker Yubbie a warm little hat? Doesn't he look cute, guys?" His buddies all egged him on, laughing like a bunch of ugly hyenas.

"Everyone should have a hat like this," he said. Then he grabbed the hat off my head. I told him to leave me alone and give me back my hat, but instead he tossed it over my head to one of his buddies.

I turned around and ran toward the kid who had my hat. Stupid move. As I neared him, he threw it over my head toward one of Vinnie's other buddies. And then he threw it to another guy. "Come on, Tubbie Yubbie," they kept saying, "come get your cute little hat." They just kept throwing it back and forth to each other, laughing at me and calling me Yubbie. I kept running round, trying to get my hat. I had to get it back. Ma would be upset if I came home without it. And then Dad would strap my hide for sure. Plus, my head and ears were getting cold. I kept on asking them to give it back and leave me alone. It must have lasted an hour—or that's the way it seemed.

That wasn't the worst of it. Across the street, a bunch of kids just stood there and watched. They didn't do a thing! I don't know what they could have done, but I wished they had done something. But no, they just stood there in perfect silence, like puppets sitting on the shelf collecting dust, and watched these jerks pick on me like I was on a TV show for their entertainment.

Finally Vinnie got the hat back. "Here Yubbie, Yubbie, Yubbie," he said, like he was calling a pig to eat. I was out of breath, and my cheeks and ears were stinging while sweat rolled down my forehead. I made a grab for my hat and he pushed me away. Then he started throwing my hat into the air trying to get it caught on the telephone peg high above him.

No! "Come on, don't do that. It's cold. I need my hat." I was begging but it didn't matter. He just kept throwing it up in the air. That's when he said he wanted to see me cry. Before the word even left his mouth, with one heaping throw he tossed my hat way up in the air. It came down on one of the telephone pole's pegs. That was it—my hat was gone. There was no way I was gonna climb the pole to get it.

I couldn't help it, I screamed "No!" louder than I ever screamed anything. Vinnie's friends looked startled or something, then they busted up and started walking away. Vinnie stayed long enough to warn me not to tell anyone. He said he'll come to my house in the middle of the night and get me if I do. "Mark my words," he said.

I looked across the street at the kids standing in front of Doll's Variety Store who had watched the whole thing. They kinda turned in another direction and just walked off—not even asking me if I was okay. That's when I started to cry. Right there underneath the telephone pole, I balled like a little girl. My humiliation was complete.

I don't understand. Doesn't anyone care? Why didn't the kids across the street go into Doll's and tell Mrs. Kusiak what was happening? She would have called the police or maybe even come out of her store with a broom and whacked Vinnie over the head or something. I felt so alone.

Life is so horrible. Life gave me this big fat body, this ugly face, these stubby hands, and not one ounce of guts. I hate life. I hate Vinnie, and I hate all his stupid buddies, and I even hate those kids across the street who didn't do a darn thing. I hate them all!

By the time I got home my ears were frozen and hurting, big time. My cheeks were burning like someone put an iron on my face. Even the top of my head hurt from the cold. Yet another reason to love the crew cut Ma makes me get. She thinks I look better in a crew cut. Like anything could make me look better.

At least I'd stopped crying by the time I got home. Only, when I walked into the house, my ma was blubbering even harder than I'd been. She was talking to someone on the phone, crying about how she doesn't know who her real mother and father are. Like usual. It never stops with her. Maybe that's why Dad doesn't talk to her much. Maybe that's all she does—cry.

She hung up the phone as I started to take off my coat and boots. She asked me where my hat was, telling me in weather like this without a hat I'd catch a cold and get sick.

That just made me start crying again. Now she'd know I lost my hat, now she'd tell Dad, now Dad would kill me. My day couldn't get any worse. She looked at me with her red eyes and asked me what was the matter and I couldn't help it, I told her I wished I was dead. She exploded. Instead of asking me what happened or why I felt that way, she said, "You better pray, boy, that you are not struck down right here, right in this spot! Go to your room and think about what you've just said. I gotta get supper ready for your dad."

I dropped my head down and fumbled up to my bedroom to cry some more. She didn't ask about my hat again, so maybe I won't get a strapping about it, but I still feel terrible inside. I can't stop shaking and I don't think it's from the cold. I'm lost. I don't know what to do. I can't talk to Ma because she just doesn't understand. If I talk to Dad about my feelings, he'll tell me, "Go and talk to your mother. She can help ya." She can't even help herself!

Life is depressing. I don't want to be here. I'm lonely, scared, and numb. Will this ever change? Maybe when I get to be an adult it will all change. Maybe I'll find a wife who will listen to me and understand what I feel. If Ma and Dad would buy me a dog for Christmas, I'd have someone to talk to and someone I could love who would love me back. There has to be a better world for me somewhere.

Maybe I should run off and join the circus and travel around the world. I could live with Hercules, the strong man, who would teach me how to lift weights. I'll bet his father didn't tell him, "What are you going to lift them with? Your belly?" I'd lose all this fat and develop mega muscles and lift a donkey with one hand, or pull a trailer truck with a harness on my head, or strap a fridge on my back and beat everyone in the Iron Man contest. People would pay big bucks just to see me do my feats of strength. I'll really become someone special and never have to worry about someone taking my hat off my head. I'd just pound him in the head with my hammer-like fist—right into the ground, with only his head sticking up. And then I'd take <u>his</u> stupid hat.

Journal Entry 11 - January 15

Talk about getting coal for Christmas—I got a mega ton. Dad tells us every year that back in his day, if he didn't behave all year, his father would put coal in his Christmas stocking as punishment. Good thing we burn oil to heat the house so there's no coal around. But Christmas still feels like one big dump of coal on my head.

I was pretty disappointed that I didn't get the German Shepard I wanted or my barbells—again—but we did get new red J jumpers. J jumpers are cool. It's like having a seat attached to a ski. I guess that's why they call them J jumpers—it looks like a J. You have to balance yourself with your feet as you sit on the seat and blast down the hill. It works great here in New England. They're the best.

I booked it over to Clifford Lane with my J jumper. Randy and Trevor stayed behind doing something, I don't even know what. A bunch of kids were there with toboggans and sleds. Our town doesn't plow that road during the winter, so we can totally blast down it. This year a couple of kids put a mound of snow in the middle to use as a jump. It was great! Man, those J jumpers flew!

But like always, I didn't get to stay airborne forever. Christmas totally crashed and burned on that hill. After about a half hour, I started another run down the hill on my J jumper when all of a sudden, BANG, BANG, BANG! I was hammered by snowballs and knocked off the J jumper. I slid down the hill on my side, barely stopping before I hit a fence.

I looked where the snowballs had come from and there was Trevor with a bunch of his little buddies. "What's the matter, Yubbie, did you fall off and go boom?"

I knew this wasn't going to be good. Once Trevor starts up he rarely backs off. I don't understand why he treats me that way.

He's such a spoiled brat. He was probably angry because I didn't ask him to come with me.

I got up from the snow bank and trudged up the steep hill. I yelled out to Trevor to cut it out and leave me alone. Big mistake. Trevor started making fun of my fat with his buddies. I tried to ignore them and finally made it to the top. I got on my J jumper and pushed off to get a fast start. But just like last time, just when I was just getting up speed, BANG, BANG, BANG! A bunch of snowballs pegged me. I didn't get knocked off this time, though. Zooming down the hill, I looked off to say something to Trevor and BANG—I hit another kid on a sled.

It was a major wreck. After I hit him I went flying through the air, only to come down on my back and slam into a couple of kids who were walking back up the hill. Then everyone came crashing down on top of me and I hurt my shoulder really bad. Trevor and his buddies were laughing and pointing.

Laying there under the pile I decided I wasn't gonna take any more from Trevor. I got back on my feet and started up the hill towards him. It was steep, so I lost my wind trying to walk quickly uphill, but I got there. Totally out of breath, I told him to leave me alone and to go home or I was going to beat him up. At first he acted like he was going to leave, and I thought, "Cool!" But then he turned real sudden and quick and shoved me in the chest. I slipped and fell backwards onto the steep hill and slid half way down. The only thing that stopped me was the snow jump—which I hit with my head. When I rolled over and looked back the top of the hill, Trevor was flying down on his J jumper, straight at me! I scrambled, but it was no use. He slid right into me and again I flew backwards, landing on my side. It really hurt.

As I lay there, Trevor walked off with his friends towards the variety store. It was like he was leaving me for dead. That was the last straw. Trevor was going to get it, big time, even if it didn't come from me: I was going to tell Dad.

I put my hat back on—Ma had threatened me with instant death if I lost this one, too—picked up my J jumper, and took off. But Trevor made it home before me and told Ma that I was picking on him. He told her that he and his friends went over to Clifford Lane to have some fun and I was threatening to beat him up after they threw a couple of harmless snowballs at me. The liar!

Ma was quick to get upset and told us to stop fighting and said that if we didn't she was going to tell Dad when he got home and then watch out! Trevor and I both knew what that meant—the strap. She told us to go watch TV, saying we couldn't get in trouble doing that.

In the living room, Trevor kept taking the remote and changing the channel I was watching. I told him to knock it off or we'd get in trouble but he kept doing it. Man, he makes me so mad! I'd switch it back to my channel only to have him change it again in a few minutes. Finally, I couldn't stand it anymore and I slugged him. The minute my fist hit his cheek I knew we were both dead. He took off for the kitchen to tell Ma. I tried to catch him to tell him, "No! Don't! She'll tell Dad!", but I can never catch Trevor. As I busted into the kitchen, Ma started yelling and tried to slap me and Trevor both just as the back door opened. Me and Trevor froze. It was Dad.

Ma launched into a rant about me and Trevor and the hill and everything, and Dad's face got redder and redder. The world stopped.

Finally, Ma was done and Dad marched right for the closet where he keeps the strap. Me and Trevor bolted. But Dad is even faster than Trevor. Throwing his coat down on the chair, he chased us to the den where he finally caught up with us. His hand went flying up in the air and the strap came down, first hitting me on the leg and then hitting Trevor in the arm. The strap stung like ten thousand bee stings at once. He just kept swinging and swinging as we cried. One hit struck me on the back and then another on my arm and still another on my butt. They were coming fast and furious. I held my hands over my face to protect it from this crazy man.

We were both crying and screaming. I tried to explain what happened on Clifford Lane. I told him that Trevor had been picking on me first and I had to do something about it, but he was in no mood to hear anything. The beating finally ended with both us on the floor crouched together like two little pigs afraid of the big bad wolf.

He told us to go to our rooms and we bolted like rockets to get out of his reach. Trevor ran upstairs, went to his bedroom, and slammed the door. I limped behind him, favoring my leg where a giant welt was blossoming.

I've tried lying on my back, but the sting of the strap hasn't faded. So now I'm just sitting here writing in my journal. None of this would have happened if Trevor had left me alone. I guess I can be happy about one thing—at least I wasn't the only one who got the beating this time.

My dad is so mean. When Ma tells us that she's going to squeal on us, shivers run down my spine. It feels like being caught in a bear trap and watching the bear come after you. You try to shrink and disappear but there's no place to hide.

Ma said this is how Grandpa disciplined my dad. So my question is, did my dad hate his dad as much as I hate him? I swear, I'll never hit my kids with a strap. One day I'll grow up to be big and strong, and then we'll see who's so tough. When Dad raises his hand to me, I'm going to stop it in mid-air just like Jean-Claude Van Damme. Then I'll bring it down to his side and hold it there while I wiggle my finger on the other hand saying, "No, no, this will <u>not</u> happen again." I won't hurt him because he's my dad, but I'll block each of his blows until he's exhausted and passes out.

I bet Danny's dad never hits him with a strap. He probably doesn't hit him at all. When I went camping with them, they seemed to like each other and enjoyed spending time together. I wish Danny's dad was my dad.That makes me terrible, I know. No way other kids hate their dads like this. Maybe I deserve the beatings.

I wish I could float away and escape this world.

Journal Entry 12 - February 17

Danny called last week telling me that if I was still interested we could join the Boy Scouts. I was excited to hear from him, and the idea of becoming a part of a group who liked the woods, camping, and hiking sounded great.

There were some requirements. I had to get a uniform, or at least a shirt with the Boy Scout insignia on it, and a couple of patches. Danny's mother offered to sew the required patches on. I also had to get a neckerchief and hat.

I was excited when Ma told me that they would buy me the shirt and that one of them would take me to the first meeting to sign the papers.

Wow! What a night.The auditorium at the hall was filled with a lot of kids joining the troop. When I walked in, I saw Danny and Tom. The last time I saw them was four months ago. Danny gives me a call sometimes just to "check in" as he calls it, but we haven't had any chances to hang out.

I still haven't figured out why he wants me to be his friend. He so smart and I'm so dumb. His dad is a lawyer and makes a lot of money and my dad works at a rolling chain plant at a machine that makes the parts of chains for forklifts. I don't think Dad makes a lot of money. He's always arguing with Ma that they don't have enough. She wants him to get another job so she can have more to spend. I'm just happy they found enough for me to join.

Maybe Danny feels sorry for me because I'm fat and nobody else wants to hang around with me? He doesn't seem like the kind of person to be that way, but otherwise I can't figure it out.

Then there's Tom. I know he hangs around with Danny because they're cousins. That makes a lot of sense. But why does he even want me to tag along? It sure isn't for my ability to play baseball. His dad is an accountant and has his own office downtown where all the banks are. He must make a lot of money too since he drives a new Subaru. We own a Chevy that's old and rusted. One of these days I'll figure it out, but for now I'm excited that they want me to be a part of the troop.

We had a lot of fun at this first meeting. After we signed the papers we were given a patrol, which is a group that we each would belong to. I got the Wildcats. Danny got the Bear cubs. Tom got the Hawks. There are about ten kids in each group. I went to my patrol and met all the scouts. There were kids of all different ages and sizes. I was the only fat one, though, and the youngest and the newest.

Some kids had all these patches—merit badges that you earn when you accomplish things. There were also different levels of Scouts, starting out as a Tenderfoot, then Second Class, First Class, Star, Life, and then the highest achievement, Eagle Scout. It's amazing, all the things you had to do to be an Eagle Scout.

For now they gave me a book with a whole bunch of things to read. Before the next meeting in a couple of weeks I have to learn the Boy Scout law by heart. Part of it says, "I am trustworthy, loyal, friendly, kind, obedient" and so on. Wouldn't that be great if everyone treated me that way?

They talked about things they were going to do, like a trip to

Camp Eagle in the Berkshires early this summer. Too bad it costs money to go. No way Ma and Dad would let me go. But then, who knows, maybe Dad will get a new job and he'll have the money. It must be beautiful there. The kids tell me there's tons to do, like hiking and swimming and stuff like that. I was a little scared when they told me about the obstacle course. I guess you have to run, jump over a log saw horse, hold onto a rope and swing over a big puddle of mud like Tarzan, and finally climb a fishing net to get to the top of some tree. I'd probably drop dead in the middle of the course. I didn't see any fat kids at the meeting tonight or in any of the patrols. I hope I didn't make a mistake.

We ended the night with my favorite cookies, soda, and ice cream. The kids were really nice. I recognized a couple of kids from my school. They came over and unfortunately said, "Hi, Yubbie." They didn't look like they were trying to insult me or say anything mean. I wonder if they believe in the pledge they took.

Anyway, I'm glad I went to the meeting. Dad told me on the way home that he wasn't going to cart me to these meetings every week. I'll have to walk or find some other means of transportation. He also told me not to expect him to get involved with the Scouts and go camping. He doesn't have the time for that stuff.

That's okay by me. I didn't want him to go camping with me anyways. I want to get away from everyone in my house, not bring them with me. At least I got what I wanted – I am now a Boy Scout and I will be able to spend some time in the woods. I can't wait, and Dad not being there is actually a good thing. No way I want someone seeing him slap me because I didn't listen, or worse, seeing him take off his belt and wale on me.

This whole Scout thing will be so cool. I can see myself now, up in the mountains, sleeping under the stars, hiking up the cliffs just like the mountain goats that Danny talked about seeing on his trip to Europe. We'll be making our way up the steep ledges in our Scout uniforms when all of a sudden we'll hear screams of fear coming from the cliff above. A troop of Girl Scouts that had been climbing this treacherous cliff ran into trouble when one slipped and fell, barely hanging on. We'll all look at each other and know what to do. We're Scouts, after all, so we're prepared. And me being the patrol leader means I've got the plan to save the girl in distress. It'll take climbing ropes and cliff tackle. I'll tell my men that a couple of us will go above the girl while the others make their way beneath her so they can catch her if she falls.

I'll lead the upper group. We'll make our way by lifting our bodies on this sheer cliff, struggling to pull ourselves up. Being the lead, I'll set the tackle hooks in the rock as a safety for the climbers below. I'll make it over to the girl, who is now crying and panicking. She can't hold on any longer, she'll say. "Don't worry," I'll tell her. "I'll be right there."

My fellow scouts will make it to my position and start lowering me over the edge just like Sylvester Stallone in "Cliffhanger." I'll lower myself just at the time when the rock she's standing on breaks loose and she'll start to fall. Fast as lightning, I'll quickly grab onto her with my one arm and pull her next to me. My men will pull us to the top. The whole way, she'll be holding on for dear life as I say, "I got ya, don't worry, you're in good hands." She'll look at me with the biggest brown eyes ever and smile.

I'll be the hero of the day. All the girls from her scout troop will circle around me and cheer and clap. The girl I saved, Nancy, will kiss me right on the cheek. What a day! I'm sure glad I joined the Scouts.

Journal Entry 13 - June 18

What a rotten way to start the summer. If today is any indication of how the rest of the summer is going to go, then I'd rather be in school. Okay, maybe that's not totally true, but still. I thought this was going to be the summer of summers! I had a lot of things planned, starting with a day at Anthony's Pool. Tom was off to baseball camp for the month and Danny was, as usual, traveling with his family. I remember how my summer ended last year and have my fingers crossed that this year will be a little different. I'm a sixth grader now, bigger than last summer. For once, that's a good thing. I was hoping my size might help ward off anyone picking on me.

I was wrong.

The day was going great. I played games, swam, and had a soda with Mary Lou. We're pretty good friends now. It's crazy, but it turns out she had some doubts about herself, just like me. Her sister is still very mean to her and constantly cuts her down. Names, mean tricks, the works. If Mary Lou makes a mistake, her sister pounces and makes fun of her.

Mary Lou doesn't approve of everything her girl friends do. They make fun of other girls and pick on them. She knows how it feels when her sister torments her and doesn't want to be a part of that stuff. Unfortunately, she wants to belong. They're the "in" crowd. So she stands back and watches them. Sometimes she wants to say something, but she's afraid they'll reject her from the group. I know about rejection. It sucks.

I don't think Mary Lou understands. She doesn't want to be rejected but just being part of this group makes her one of them—the ones who pick on people. I know about not wanting to be rejected but I have a hard time with the watching part. I think she'd be better off without those friends. Maybe I can change her mind.

Things were going fine with me and Mary Lou at the pool. But then, like a passing summer thunderstorm coming out of nowhere, Vinnie and the boys showed up. I turned my head and there they were. My heart started racing, my forehead got all sweaty, and my whole body felt like it was sinking. I was about to be attacked by a pit bull.

I didn't make eye contact and just kept trying to talk to Mary Lou. Vinnie talks like he swallowed a bullhorn, though, so I could hear him. He said, "Hey, let's sit down with Yubbie and have a chat." Then of course they beelined it over to me. "You don't mind a little visit, do ya, Fatso?"

Yes!! I should've said it out loud, though, not thought it. Now he was trying to embarrass me in front of Mary Lou. All I had the guts to say was, "Leave me alone." That worked about as well as waving a bone in front of a starving dog and telling him not to eat it. Vinnie slapped me in the back of my head, making my nose almost hit the table.

Mary Lou screamed at him to leave me alone. Now my humiliation was complete. Everything Vinnie said back at her is burned into my mind. He said,"What do you see in this fat slob? He looks like a hippo out of water."Then he said,"Yubbie is so fat he reminds me of the Michelin tire boy. He's got layers and layers of fat rolling everywhere. Sometimes I think I should call him Yubbie Sweet Potato Pie."

The room started spinning and I couldn't see right and all I wanted to do was run away and never stop running. It was like he wanted to see how far he could push me before I exploded or something. I tried to leave, but he put his hand on my shoulder and slammed me back down on the picnic table.

Then he said,"Listen, fat man, this is my territory and it's off limits to Yubbie."And he slapped me in the head again! "I don't want to see you back here again.This is the only warning you're gonna get. Next time you show your face at Anthony's, you're dead meat. I'll take you in the woods and beat you within an inch of your life. I'll pound you so hard that all the fat will drop right off your bones. Understand?"

Then, the big, fat chicken that I am, I nodded. That's it. He threatened to almost kill me and I just nodded. Can you get any more pathetic than that? When he left, Mary Lou tried to tell me I should tell someone and not let him treat me that way. I already tried that! My parents don't listen! Mary Lou doesn't get it. No one does. Dad just tells me it takes a bigger man to walk away than fight. But I can't walk away. I get slapped back down into my seat when I do. I don't know what to do!

So, I'll just do what I'm told. I'll stay away from Anthony's.Wild horses couldn't drag me back there.

I'm so sick and tired of this torture. I wish it could be different. It should be like the law of the jungle.Tarzan would know what to do. I could be like him.A raging wild rhino with Vinnie's ugly face could be charging and I, like Tarzan, would just stare him right in the eyes. No fear.The rhino would approach, closer and closer, grunting and huffing, exhaling each breath with such force that the air from its nostrils bursts the grains of sand from the ground, and I wouldn't even blink.

With the rhino just about on me, I'd jump to the side and leap on its back and ride it like a bronco. I'd pull out my knife and start stabbing the rhino in the back of its neck. Rhinos have thick skin, though, so it would take all my strength to penetrate its exterior. My knife would take its toll as blood would gush out and down its back.

Finally, the rhino would collapse, submitting to my strength and force. I'd look deep into the eyes of the dying wild beast, wondering why it charged me. We both would've been happy if it had just gone on its merry way. Even though it was bigger, stronger, and faster than me, courage and confidence won. It's the law of the jungle—only the strongest survive, and today the strongest was me.

Journal Entry 14 - July 7

Today was confusing. I thought it was bad enough being picked on 'cause I'm fat, bad enough being called Yubbie, but today something happened that has me boggled. Someone hates me because I'm Polish. That's a new one.

The day started out okay, my fourth day at Camp Eagle. The first two days were great. I did all kinds of new things. I learned how to tie knots, lash branches to make a chair with rope, and go on nature hikes having a guide show us different kind of plants and animals in the woods. I even saw that poison ivy stuff Danny's father showed us. Everything was so exciting.

Things got a little tricky on the third day when we had Field Day. It was just like the scouts told me at the meeting. We had to run a relay, jump over a log sawhorse, hold onto a rope and swing over a pool of water, and finally climb up a cargo net—not a fish net—to its top and down the other side. All the other scouts gave the obstacle course a shot. Some did really well, but even some of the scouts who were in shape had a hard time. One guy who was swinging over the water missed the edge of the pool and slipped, falling part way in the mud. He grabbed onto the edge and pulled himself up and acted like he was fine.

If he did that, what would happen when it was my turn? I didn't want to say no because that would bring a lot of attention to me. So I just waited my turn. I noticed none of the scouts were as fat as me. Some of them were skinny and tall, but no real hippos.

I was up next. I never did anything like this before. I almost turned and ran the wrong way on purpose, but then I didn't. I took that need to run and pointed myself forward. First I ran and picked up the relay stick and returned it to the next staging area. I was out of breath halfway there and struggled to make it, more walking fast than running near the end.

Next was jumping over the log sawhorse. Most kids ran up to the horse and put two hands on the top then hurled their two legs over. I even saw one kid jump right on top of the horse, land on his feet, and then jump over. Incredible! It looked easy. I ran up to the horse breathing really hard, placed my two hands on its back, and jumped as high as I could. Big surprise: I totally face planted. My jump wasn't high enough, so I crashed into the horse, falling over it head first. I have a pretty good scrape on my cheek now. The horse didn't move, which was lucky, I guess. I didn't end up trapped.

One of the counselors bent over and asked me if I was all right. I told him I tripped before I got to the sawhorse. He nodded a lot, saying, "Yeah, yeah, bad luck," but I don't think he believed me. He told me I could stop if I wanted. I said, "I'm good, I'm good. Ready to go!" even though I wasn't. My back hurt and my cheek burned, big time. But it would hurt even more to walk right off the middle of the course after that maneuver. I pointed myself to the mud pit and ran forward.

A counselor was holding the swing rope for me. I took the rope and ran as fast as I could off the edge. And there's where my next problem was: I thought for a second I could actually do this. I thought I was Tarzan. But about halfway across, my hands gave way. I fell right in the middle of the water, which was definitely more like mud. Totally caked in mud, I sat on my butt listening to some of the other kids laugh.

I thought about sitting there and crying. I thought about getting up and running off the course. But something in me refused to do either of those things. I'm a Scout now. Scouts don't run away. I got to my feet as a counselor ran in the mud to give me a hand. "Are you all right?" he asked. "Of course I am," I said as I got to my feet. I didn't even take his hand. I could do this.

He told me to take a break and wash up. I could come back later, he said. But I couldn't stop. There were too many kids around. I couldn't give up. I had to show them that I could do it. I'm a Scout just like them.

I showed him my muddy hands. "My hands were slippery and I lost my grip. I'm okay." Then I ran past him. He didn't stop me.

Here comes the piece de resistance. That's means finale. Danny taught it to me.

I started up the cargo net, almost totally wiped out by this point. It was like my arms and legs were noodles. I tried to pull myself up but had a real hard time finding a place to put my feet. Plus, the net moved forward every time I tried to place my foot in a hole, which means I'd end up hanging by my arms with my legs flapping all over. Whenever I finally did get my feet placed, I was rocking like a teeter-totter. "I'm a Scout," I kept saying to myself, but it was no use. I'm so uncoordinated I just couldn't do it. Finally my hands let go and I fell backwards, catching my feet in the ropes and ending up hanging upside down. The group went hysterical and I thought I might as well just die right there. The counselors were yelling at the kids to knock it off as they tried to support me and get me upright by untangling my feet.

I couldn't believe it was happening. It took four counselors to get me loose. They were all very nice, and one escorted me to the medical building. A male nurse checked me out to see if I was hurt. I tried to tell him I was okay and nothing was broken. My back was really sore and my ankles had burns on them, but so what? It ain't any worse than a beating from Dad. The thing is, I got this way trying. Trying. I didn't wimp out and run away. Even though I hurt all over, I was kind of proud, in a weird way. Not that I ever want to do another obstacle course.

Still, I knew that if I went outside again everyone would make fun of me and tease me. So when the counselor suggested I return to my campsite and report to my adult group leader, I did. He said to take a shower and get cleaned up. "Tomorrow is another day, Scout." Seriously, he called me, "Scout."

I woke up this morning feeling pain. In fact, it hurt more than the strap. My adult leader suggested I skip activities today. It was going to be another field day and he wanted to make sure I didn't get hurt. I agreed, knowing that my body couldn't stand another day of this torture. And I was still kind of feeling proud, almost, for at least finishing the course yesterday.

I reported to a counselor in charge of maintenance. My job was to give him a hand for the day. My group leader told me it was going to be easy. I was introduced to Pierre. He was going to show me what to do. He was from my hometown, but he lives in an entirely different neighborhood.

As soon as we started to walk away he asked me, "Your last name sounds like you're Polish?" I didn't see how that mattered for anything, so I just said, "Yes." "I hate Polacks," he spat out. I was floored. I didn't know what to say. "You people are trouble no matter where you are. Now you're at camp and giving me a pain 'cause I have to baby-sit for a retarded Polack. It stinks. I had other plans, but if I got to have you with me then I have plenty of important work for you."

He was much older than me, much taller and stronger. He was a counselor. What was I going to say? No? I don't know what they do in the Scouts, but on a TV show I saw an army guy in battle say no to his captain, and the captain shot him in the head. I thought for a minute, remembering that Camp Eagle had a shooting range. I didn't say a word.

He gave me latrine duty, telling me that because Polacks stink this was the right job for me. I went around camp putting toilet paper in all the outside toilets and washing the seats with this blue disinfectant. He was right. The latrines stank. I cussed at him in my thoughts as I went from toilet to toilet. What did the Polish people do to the French to deserve cleaning toilets? I didn't even know him! He didn't know me! His anger was based on my nationality. I'm a Scout and he's a Scout . . . doesn't that matter? I was totally confused, but after all the problems I caused the day before during field exercise, I wasn't gonna rock the boat.

So now I'm a dumb stinking Polack. As if it wasn't bad enough that I'm fat and called Yubbie. Here I was finally having people call me "Scout" like they were proud that I was, and then this guy comes and ruins it. It's not right. How did I come to this earth? Was I born with a sign on my back that says "Kick me!" or something? Living really sucks sometimes. I joined the Scouts to have fun, and scrubbing toilets is <u>not</u> fun. What happened to the pledge we repeat every day in camp? Doesn't Pierre mean it when he says that pledge?

Some day I'm going to become an Eagle Scout and hold the Order of the Arrow and every award the Scouts offer. Then I'll be a leader here at this camp. I'll have everyone repeat the pledge every day and watch to see how they behave. Scouts who only speak the words but don't act respectful will have to answer to me. People will have great respect for me as a leader because I'll make everyone hold to the pledge. Anyone who violates the pledge will be disciplined. I would cast them out into the woods with no survival equipment in an area where there are mountain lions and grizzly bears. It would only have to happen once where the wild animals ate someone up, and then no one would violate the pledge.

I think I'm going ask Dad about this Polack stuff.

Journal Entry 15 - July 14

I wonder if there's any hope for me. I'm such a loser. I can't do anything and I don't know why.

I was happy that Ma and Dad bought me a guitar for my birthday even though it was the wrong kind. I started taking lessons the week after I got it. I went to the music shop where Ma bought it. I had to. The owner's name is Mr. Coachtree. I know we started off on the wrong foot because I blamed him for telling Ma which guitar to buy. But after the wrong foot, it just kept getting worse. I really didn't like him as a teacher. He tried to make me play corny songs that are old and babyish, like "Row, Row, Row Your Boat." Am I in kindergarten or something? At first I tried not to let it bother me since I was learning, but what I really want is to learn the songs I hear on the radio.

He told me to practice every day, and I do. Randy tells me that I sound terrible. He says it sounds like my guitar is out of tune and I'm making eerie vibrations that send chills down his spine. He keeps telling me that the neighbors are going to complain to the police because it sounds like somebody is dying in our house. He also told me that some guys in white jackets will be coming to take me away to the funny farm for trying to impersonate a musician. He laughs at me and tells me to stop annoying him with the racket.

Trevor is no better. He keeps telling me to give it up and he howls like a dog when I'm playing. He says it helps drown out the sour notes I hit and maybe the rest of the dogs in the neighborhood will join in the concert. He thinks I should start a band called The Howlers.

The only one who says anything good is Ma, and I know she's just saying that to be nice. Dad? Well, I don't think he even knows I practice, or if he does, he never listens to me. I really don't think he cares what I do or how I'm doing.

I thought it would be a lot easier. I keep trying and trying, but my fingers don't move the way I want them to. Maybe I have some rare medical problem that affects the way my brain communicates to my hands. I asked Ma if I could try another teacher because I didn't like Mr. Coachtree. I thought he wasn't giving me the right kind of music to learn, and she agreed. Maybe she didn't like my playing very much, either.

I'd heard that there was another teacher up by Uncle Wally's house. That teacher plays in his own band and has been playing his whole life. He's supposed to be really good. Everyone says he is a great teacher. Ma agreed to let me switch to him since he charges the same price per lesson as Mr. Coachtree does.

I was so excited. I knew that he was going to be the right teacher and I'd learn the type of music I liked. Maybe he would invite me to play in his band? Wouldn't that be cool, teacher and student playing together in the same band and becoming famous?

The first day I arrived for my lesson, I was late. Mr. Kottie was a little upset. He asked me to show him what I could do. I took my guitar and tried to play the sheet music in front of me. It was hard. He asked me how long I'd been playing. I told him it had been nine months. He told me that I would have to start from scratch. Shoot! Not what I wanted to hear. I mean, I don't sound

<u>that</u> bad. And what if he's right and I do still suck after nine months? Is there something wrong with me?

He gave me new music and instructions. At least he was nice enough to ask me what kind of music I like and wanted to learn. I chose one of my favorites, <u>Times Like These by the Foo Fighters.</u> I practiced every day. It's been over a month with Mr. Kottie and today he told me that my tempo is off. He started me with a machine that makes a sound like a clock. He called it a metronome. He wanted me to play the beat at the speed of the clicker. I was so nervous. I couldn't do it. It just didn't come out right at all.

After the lesson Mr. Kottie told me that I might want to consider another hobby, instrument, or sport. He doesn't believe I can play a guitar! He told me that playing guitar comes easier to some and because I had a hard time keeping the tempo he thought I might want to consider something else.

I felt really sad when I left his house. Why was I born so stupid? Why am I such a retard? I just keep failing at everything I want to do. I don't know why.

Randy is really good with building things. Trevor is now on a little league team and even hit a home run. But me, Yubbie, I'm fat and useless. No matter how much I try, I can't seem to do anything right. I'll probably catch a lightning bolt in the back of my head for even writing this, but I wish I was never born. Really! It would've been better for me. I think something happened in birth. Maybe I came out the wrong way, or maybe the doctor dropped me on my head and something got loose. That's what Randy says. He says something happened to make me this way. I'm not happy.

I wish I could stop crying, but the tears just keep coming. I'm like a leaky faucet. I'm so confused and sad. I'm lonely and I'm tired. I don't know what to do. I hate my life, my face, and this fat body. Something happened to me and no one wants to tell me the truth. I'm probably going to stay like this forever.

Maybe I should just stop taking lessons. The teachers don't want to help me learn. Who needs tempo, anyway? I'll bet Jimmy Hendrix never took a lesson, and he was one of the best guitarists in the world. I'll show everybody. I'll learn how to play on my own. I'll go on "American Idol" and get famous and then they'll all see that I'm someone. I'll be the best!

People will flock to my concerts. Girls will scream and go crazy. Millions will beg for my autograph. I'll have my chauffeur drive my stretch limo up to Mr. Kottie's house. I'll get out and knock on his door. I'll bring a copy of my latest platinum album with my autograph on the cover. When he comes to the door, I'll smile and say, "See, I'm the best. I did it." And then I'll break the album over his head and laugh. He'll eat his words.

Journal Entry 16 - August 1

I love picnics. Dad and Ma took all of us to White Birch today for a Sunday picnic. A bunch of our neighbors were there enjoying the hot summer day. Everyone gets together in the same area to eat, drink, and laugh. They all like to play a card game called Polish Pitch. I'll bet there weren't any French people invited to this picnic.

I took a chance today to talk to Dad. Randy was helping Ma get the food ready and Dad asked me if I wanted to go to the pavilion and change into my bathing suit with him. I rarely get a chance to be alone with him so I agreed. I told him what happened to me with the French counselor at Camp Eagle. I was kind of afraid he'd get mad at me, like I did something to bring on the latrine duty, but he didn't. He actually talked to me, really talked.

He tried to explain why the French counselor at Camp Eagle

was so mean to me. He said years ago the French and Polish settled in our little town to work in the cotton mills but they decided to live in different areas. For some reason they didn't have anything to do with each other, but he didn't know exactly why. He told me if a French person called a Polish person a Polack then fists would start flying. All over a name? I know I get upset at people calling me Yubbie, but these are adults—they're not supposed to fight.

Dad said that more than once when he was young he got into brawls with French guys. Back then he called them Frogs. Funny, neither of us could figure out why they called them Frogs. Maybe it's because they eat frog legs? Anyway, the way he explained it was, if someone called you a Frog or a Polack, you punched them in the nose and tried to tear their head off. It was all because they had different nationalities that they hated each other.

Dad told me that Polack is the Polish word for a guy and Polka is for a female. That makes sense, I guess, but I don't see why you're supposed to get insulted if they're using the words the right way. It sounded like you could only use the word Polack if you were Polish—any other nationality, and BAM! SLAM! I don't get it. It must be like a black person calling another black person the "n" word and it's okay, but if a white person uses the "n" word then the black person is mad. People are confusing.

Dad was super mad that the French counselor treated me that way. He told me that if he'd known about it while I was at camp, he would've smacked "the Frog" in the head and reported the incident to the camp authorities. Seriously, he was ticked. He was tired that we still had to put up with this type of crap. Part of me wished I'd never brought it up 'cause he got so red in the face. Now I know why I don't tell my parents the truth. They get so mean.

Later that day Randy had his chance to get mean. A bunch of kids who were part of our picnic group were at the beach sitting on their blankets taking in some sun and having a good time. All of a sudden Randy looked at me and said, "You're starting to look like a girl. You better start losing some of that fat or you'll need a bra, bro!"

He made me feel awful. Even my brother, someone who's supposed to love me, hates me. Trevor and Randy laughed it off while I sat there numb and speechless, shooting him a stare that could stop a freight train as everyone else had a good chuckle.

Finally I just got up and walked into the water, right up to my neck. At least the people in the water couldn't tell what I look like. Just being in the lake erased some of the hurt. I swim fast and can hold my breath for a long time underwater. I love it there.

I wish prejudice didn't exist. Why can't people just get together and love each other? Why do they have to be so mean? Randy and the French counselor just don't get it. Everything they say tears me apart inside and makes me hate myself.

It could be different. People should all get together like they do for the pancake breakfast every year on Main Street. Everybody comes. It doesn't matter if you're black, yellow, red, or purple, or wear hats like turbans. Everybody comes and nobody is turned away.

I can see it now. The streets would be barricaded off with tables stretching for miles and miles. Everybody would be invited and we'd all sit down to the biggest pancake breakfast in the world. People would be there from every country, every church, every neighborhood, and every color. No one would be left out.

When they arrive I would meet them at the gate and hug them or shake their hands, telling them how welcome they are and how happy I am to see them. I would tell them that they're loved and that each one of them is very special.

They could have any kind of pancake they dreamed of.

They could have butterscotch rock pancakes, my favorite, or strawberry banana, blueberry, buttermilk, chocolate chip, and even a Belgian Waffle. Anything. All they had to do would be promise to shake everybody's hand around them and give every other person a hug.

Is that so hard? The world would be such a better place if everybody loved everybody and it didn't matter if you were fat from eating all the different pancakes or if you were from China. Everybody just accepted everybody with open arms. Everybody would be part of one big happy family. Wouldn't that be great? Maybe someday!

Maybe someday everybody will love me and be nice to me.

Journal Entry 17 - August 15

I'm crying as I write in my journal tonight. But tonight it's because I'm happy. I was just presented first place at the campfire, receiving ten world-class jamboree patches for being Scout of the Day! I can't believe it! Me! I won! Wow! How can it be? I hope they didn't give it to me because they felt sorry for me.

It all started when Tom and Danny suggested that we participate in the summer's last camping event for the local Boy Scout troops. It was a big one. Over six troops would be there competing in a bunch of different events. It sounded great and I got permission from Ma and Dad to go.

It was a tough start. We had to hike ten miles up a mountain the first day to our campsites. We had to wear a knapsack with over thirty pounds of equipment. We had to take tents, pots, pans—everything. It was a lot to carry. I was hoping I'd be able to keep up with the rest of the scouts.

As the hours started to add up, my legs began to burn. We'd stop every now and then, but when we started up again my legs would burn even more.

We came upon a swampy area and trudged through the mud. Everyone had to lift their legs high to get their feet out of the mud to take the next step. My legs ached and burned like someone was putting acid on them.

I just kept going. "I can do it, I can do it." The more it burned, the more I repeated it in my mind. I had to keep up. I couldn't stop or make anyone else stop. I couldn't wait for the next break.

We finally stopped and were told we were one hour away from our destination. I drank my water wondering how my legs were going to carry me up the next ridge. They were shaking, going into spasm. It took minutes before I could catch my breath. My shoulders were sore and my back hurt. I felt like I might pass out or like maybe if I laid down I would fall asleep.

It seemed like the break just started when it was time to get up and continue the hike. I don't even know how I managed to stand up. Then, when I pulled on my backpack, my back exploded in pain. Between that and the fire in my legs, I was pretty much toast. I wondered if you could die from a hike.

All the guys around me looked tired, that's for sure. But no one looked like he was going to die. I made up my mind that I had to finish the hike with all my equipment on my back. I must have repeated, "I can do it" a hundred thousand times, or even a million.

Finally, we hit home base. I don't think I could have walked another step. It felt like my legs were going to fall off. All I could think about was sleep. The scout leaders had other plans.

We had to set up camp. We had to put up our tents, get pine branches for our bedding, gather firewood, and get water. No one was going to make fun of me this day, not if I could help it. I was like a machine. "I can do it, I can do it. . . ." I was totally dizzy and thought I'd puke most of the time, but I did do it. I did!

It was getting dark by the time we were done, and all the troops started their campfires. For the first time in my life, I wasn't hungry. We had beans and hot dogs. Normally I can chow down a half dozen dogs in the blink of an eye, but that night I was so tired I barely ate one.

When the bugle finally played for lights out, I almost jumped up and cheered. Only, I was too tired, so I just thought about cheering. I don't even remember getting into my sleeping bag.

The next time I heard the bugle, I almost cried. Already time to wake up? The torture! Just opening my eyes made my body scream in pain. My feet had blisters, my back ached, and my legs were stiff. You'd think Vinnie or Randy just beat me up.

We all joined in getting ready for the day. We had a nice big breakfast—nothing better than slab bacon, scrambled eggs, and Texas toast cooked on the open fire. And bug juice, can't forget the bug juice. After skipping dinner the night before, that stuff really hit the spot. Next we had to clean up the campsite for inspection. I made extra sure my tent and equipment were perfect. Everything was in order.

I looked at the activity roster for the day. There were twenty different activities we could compete in. The first item on the list was field exercises. Yeah, right! No way was I signing up for that one. There were a bunch of other options. There was building a fire with a bow drill or flint and steel. You could prepare a campsite, make a lariat, or lash furniture. It's been nine months since I became a Scout. I have read most of the outdoor manual. It's really interesting. At our weekly meetings and weekend camp outings we've been learning and practicing these skills. Most of the kids just want to do the physical things. I think learning these skills are dope and put in a lot of practice not only when I am with the troop but when I hike alone up the Tofic River. I knew I could do those well and signed up for a number of them.

The first was starting a fire with bow drill. Davy Crocket would've used one. It's kinda simple. There is a bow and a stake. You wrap the leather bowstring around the stake and slide the bow back and forth like crazy. That makes heat at the bottom of the stake that makes the block of wood it's resting on get hot. That makes the straw glow red. Just a puff of breath on the straw and, like magic, it bursts into flame. I practiced it many times before and it was easy once you got the hang of it. The trick was to get really dry hay or straw that'll burn easily.

The Boy Scout manual tells you to always be prepared. I started carrying around a pouch of stuff when I walk in the woods at home. You never know when you might need some straw, a knife, or a couple candy bars. I've been practicing for months on my own. I would always prepare my fires next to the Tofic River just to play it safe.

Next I got permission to try the flint and steel, too. I had everything I needed in my day bag. I was prepared. In the last nine months I have gone from Tenderfoot to Second Class. I really like this scouting stuff. Building fires is one of the first things you have to learn as a Scout. You never know when you might get lost in the woods and have to use your survival skills. I take no chances. I want to be like Daniel Boone. I wish school was this easy.

Taking out my own steel and flint, I struck my flint several times to ignite the straw and cloth. Then I brought the straw to my face and gently blew until the embers burst into flames.

I was so happy and excited. There are things I can do better than other people? Who would've guessed? Being prepared really works.

I had completed all my tasks. A counselor came around and looked at the campsite I prepared and took notes. I even had time to sit back and chow at my site. All the other kids were too busy running relays and jumping over horses and swinging over mud and stuff. Me? I'd rather sit on the hillside watching the butterflies and birds while munching a nice chocolate cake with fudge frosting and drinking a glass of bug juice.All I would need to make it perfect would be my guitar. It would be just great to sit back and strum a few songs.That's way better than falling into mud.

I had a blast. I had learned how to make tight lashing and I made a chair and small table. That took me forever—a whole hour and a half—but it came out just right.

Before I knew it, the day was done and it was time for supper. We had beef stew, just like you would see on the cowboy movies. I ate a couple of bowls, it was so good. Everyone was having such a great time.

After dark all the troops gathered around the main campfire. They had counselors dressed in Indian outfits and war paint. One started dancing around the unlit fire chanting Indian words and sprinkling a little dust on the logs—and the logs burst into flames! Wow! Really cool. One of the braves started singing "Kumbaya," and all the troops joined it. It was fantastic.

Time for the awards. I never even gave it a thought. All the other scouts were way better at stuff than me.There were a lot of points given to the field exercises, and I didn't do any of those, so why would I think I could receive anything?

The head counselor read off the third place award then the second place and when he said, "The first place winner and Scout of the Day goes to Joe," I nearly melted into the ground. I thought I was dreaming. Tears filled my eyes as I tried to make it to my feet. My legs felt like lead as I struggled to get up. Me! I walked to the front and the counselor who gave me the box with the patches congratulated me, saying, "Joe has shown outstanding Scouting skills in starting a campfire, cooking, lashing, and, most importantly, being prepared." I couldn't hold the tears back. I was somebody today. I can't believe it. Tom and Danny ran over to congratulate me. What an awesome night!

Journal Entry 18 - August 27

How can you go from feeling like you're worth something to feeling like you're worthless? The summer is almost over and things were going so good since I stopped going to Anthony's Pool. It's been a little over a week since I received the Scout of the Day award. I was so proud of myself. I had accomplished something. I bragged to everyone about it. But today it all tanked.

A bunch of kids who hung around the school asked me to play football on Sierra Street today. They told me that I'd be perfect for the game—I'm big and would make a good tackle, they said. It sounded like fun. I watch football on TV and thought I'd give it a try.

There were two teams and we agreed that we were only going to play for fun. My team put me right in the middle. My job was to get the quarterback or protect our quarterback from getting hit. Easy.

The kids playing were my age and I was the biggest. The game was going great even though I had a hard time catching my breath between plays. The big players on TV go over to the sidelines and breathe from an oxygen tank to recover, but of course we don't have that.

I was doing good. I could stop the oncoming players by putting my shoulders down and pushing as hard as I could with my legs. I knocked down so many players. Wow! I thought, "I can do this." They fell like dominos when I smashed into their line.

We were having a great time. We decided to take a break and were sitting around talking when I spotted Vinnie and his buddies coming down the street. I can't even guess why he was in <u>this</u> neighborhood, in <u>this</u> park. I used to walk here to go to the Tofic River because I knew I could avoid them. They usually hung out on the other side of the river.

Vinnie had a red plastic baseball bat, and one of his crew was tossing a Wiffle ball in the air, so I guess they were going to play baseball. I figured I'd be safe, though, since I was with a whole bunch of kids. And things really did look cool for a while there, with Vinnie and his guys playing over in one part of the park and us over in a different corner. But then one of Vinnie's buddies hit the ball right into the area where we were still sitting for our break. One of his other buddies ran over to pick the ball up and noticed me talking to my new friends. He yelled out, "Hey, Vinnie, guess who's here? It's your good old fat friend, Yubbie."

No! It was so unfair! A dark cloud was about to come overhead and dump hail stones on my head. I couldn't believe that even with all the other kids around, Vinnie was going to take the chance and pick on me. I thought maybe if he comes over, my new friends would stand up for me and take on Vinnie and his boys. Heck, we were teammates. That's what teammates are supposed to do for each other—cover each other's backs.

Wrong on both counts. Vinnie and his boys did come over and they did start ripping on me. By this time I was used to his insults and figured he was only going to embarrass me. I thought quick, stood up, and said, "Break's over! Who's got the ball?" hoping that everyone would stand up and start moving toward the field and maybe distract the moment. To my surprise everybody just sat there like lumps on a log watching the play unfold.

As soon as I got up, like receivers running for a Hail Mary pass, Vinnie and his boys were around me and stopped me from moving. I felt a chill knowing the storm was about to break. I looked at all my new friends on the ground and not one of them moved. I couldn't believe it! Didn't they know what was going to happen? Didn't they realize that these guys were about to trash me?

Vinnie was holding the bat. I tried to tell him that all I wanted to do is leave and then I started walking backward toward the river. He started to twirl the bat in his hand like a baton. I knew it was a plastic Wiffle bat, but still, it was a bat. I didn't like the look of him with that thing in his hand. Up to now he'd pushed me around, but I never thought he'd hit me. He said, "I told you this is my town, Fatso, and I never wanted to see you anywhere around me. You just don't listen. You must be stupid and can't get it through your fat head. It's time for someone to pound it into that thick skull."

There are no words to describe the amount of fear I felt. He was going to beat me like he'd promised, and he was going to use the bat. Vinnie turned to all the kids I was playing with and said, "If any of you want a beating just stick around. Otherwise, buzz off. Now!"

They all started to stand up and walk away. It was insane! They left me alone to get thrashed. I was about to yell at them not to go when BAM!, the red bat came smashing on my right leg. It stung like a thousand bees attacking. I begged Vinnie to stop but he just kept hitting my left leg. All his buddies were laughing, coaching him to hit a homerun. My arms, my back, the back of my legs—he pounded whatever he could get at.

I fell down to the ground and covered my face and started crying and yelling. "Stop, please stop." But this only made him swing harder. He kept slamming me with the bat—I swear it went on for an hour, at least! When he finally stopped, he was out of breath and panting. "You now understand, Fat Man. Keep away from me. Leave town. There's no room for you here." He handed the bat to one of his buddies. They walked off laughing about the bat being dented and cracked.

So there I was, just lying on the ground. I could've been dead, for all anyone cared. There was no one in sight. The other kids had left the park while I was being turned into a human Wiffle ball. I lay on the ground looking into the sky, relieved that it was over. I had some welts on my legs, but nothing was broken as far as I could tell. Dad's given it to me much worse than that. What's a little stinging from a stupid plastic bat compared to the strap?

Still, I'd been beaten up like some stupid dog, and in front of a whole bunch of guys. I cried all the way home. No one stood up to Vinnie, no one called for help, no one did anything. Why not? Why not?!

I feel so empty. It's like there's no emotion inside of me. I've been staring at the wall in my bedroom for a while now. I don't want to go downstairs for dinner. I don't want to eat, I don't want to watch TV, I don't want to play my guitar, I don't want to do anything. I don't feel like I'm alive. Maybe they were right to leave me for dead in that park. Serves me right for having some fun. What business did I have playing football? It's sad, though. I was actually pretty good at it. Maybe if they would've stood up for me, I could've played with them all the time, and then maybe get good enough to go pro.

I can see in my mind a football game. I'm a linebacker like Teddy Bruscki of the Patriots and Vinnie is the quarterback for the opposing team. It's the Super Bowl—and my chance to pay off an old debt.

We set up on the line. Vinnie sees me behind the tackles. The empty stare in my eyes rocks him to the core. I know he can sense the fury in my heart, the hatred radiating from my body. I'm going to smash him—smash him BAD—and he knows it. I can sense his fear, like the fear I felt today. He knows he's dead meat.

"Hike!" The ball is snapped, and like a herd of wild stallions,

I crush through the line and chase Vinnie as he drops back to throw the ball. The sucker doesn't even see me coming! He raises his hand to pass and POW!, I'm crashing into his chest. He's hurled backward five feet in the air, my body following as we both hit the ground with teeth-smashing force. You can hear a groan and gush of air coming out of his mouth as he's slammed into the ground.

I get up with ease, not offering him a hand. The wind is knocked out of him, so he wheezes and looks real shaken up. He's shocked at the force that buried him. He finally gets to his feet and tries to brush off what happened. Little does he realize that the game has just begun and I'm feeling like a Spartan ready to take on the Persian army like in the movie "300."

Play after play, quarter after quarter, I cut right through their line, crushing Vinnie over and over until his ability to brush it off starts to weaken. One time he's helped off the field by the medical team, totally dazed. Everyone is curious if he's going to come back.

This is my day of revenge. Payback is merciless. I cheer at the news that he's returning to play. Another chance to devastate him!

With thirty seconds on the play clock in the fourth quarter, my team is ahead by seven and Vinnie is on our ten-yard line. As I set up, I know that it's time to end his career in pro football here and now, on this last play. It's time to bury Vinnie. He's not going to get up.

I set up, feeling empty. It's like there's no emotion inside of me—I'm detached from the world. All business, baby. I don't care that I'm in a packed stadium, I don't care that my teammates are screaming or that there's music playing. All I can see is Vinnie.

The ball is snapped and I jump over the opposing tackles and fly into Vinnie—my shoulder burying deep into his gut in the blink of an eye. He didn't see it coming. He'd just started to move backward. The force blows him ten yards back, with me like a bullet embedded in him. We land so hard his eyeballs seem to pop out of his head. He goes silent. The last thing he remembers is me getting up and looking him square in the eyes as he blacks out. I dust my hands off like I just finished taking out the trash.

The medical team carries him off the field in a stretcher. I feel great knowing that I gave him all the pain he gave me over the years—plus some. I feel no pity, just delight. He had no regrets for me all those years, and I have none for him now.

Later in the day I'm watching the news and hear that football quarterback Vinnie is in critical condition at the local hospital. He hasn't regained consciousness and is suspected of having sustained a serious back and head injury. Recovery is questionable. I smile in satisfaction. Now he understands.

Journal Entry 19 - September 16

Life is sweet.There are times when the stars from above sprinkle their magic dust on the earth and everything turns beautiful. I had my first kiss. Wow! Incredible! Turn my head around, do a double take. It happened. It really happened!

Mary Lou and I have been friends for over a year. I enjoy spending time with her. I feel special when she's around. She doesn't always talk about herself but wants to talk about me, too.

She told me she was proud of me when I received the Scout of the Day Award and said, "See, I told you. You have talent." She takes the time to talk about the future and all the possibilities in life. She's a dreamer like me. She likes the woods and enjoys looking at nature, too. We have so much in common. She even asked me if I'd play my guitar for her some time. Well, I try not to stretch things too much with her but I don't think I'm ready to give a concert. I practice, but practice hasn't made me perfect yet. Sometimes I hate myself for letting people believe I'm something I'm not.

I was totally surprised one day when she told me that she'd decided not to hang with the football groupies anymore. She told me that she couldn't just stand there and watch them be mean to other kids anymore. It wasn't worth being part of the "in crowd." She knew what it was like to be picked on and hated it. I think that maybe seeing me humiliated by Vinnie's group might have played a part in changing her mind. I hope so.

She told me that she made new friends at school and tries to avoid the other girls. Now they say stuff to her, but she walks away and doesn't pay any attention to them. Or at least she doesn't let them know that she's being hurt by what they say. Sometimes I wish I could do that. If it was just words, I probably could.

I decided to go to the movies today. It was Sunday and rainy—not much to do outside. I noticed that the movie "Wall-E" was showing at the theater downtown. I really wanted to see it. Usually I'm stuck going with Trevor. I won't sit with that jerk, but Ma won't let him go alone so I end up being the watchdog for the jackal. I lucked out today. Trevor went over to a buddy's house for the afternoon. Cool! The jackal found another carcass to gnaw on.

I was in the lobby at the theater when I noticed Mary Lou standing in line at the concession stand. Wow! I wondered what was she doing by herself? I didn't see anyone with her so I looked around. There weren't any familiar faces from our school that she would hang around with.

I went over and said hi and asked her what's up. She told me that she had a big argument with her older sister this morning and just had to get out of the house. She didn't even think of calling her friends, she just took off and decided to go to the movies. She needed something to make her laugh.

I asked her, if she didn't mind could I sit with her? She told me she would be happy to have my company. Before we left the concession stand I made sure to stock up on the goodies and have enough just in case Mary Lou wanted some. She just bought a soda and small popcorn—I went on a shopping spree. Can't watch a movie without the necessities! With our hands full of goodies, we trudged our way into the movie.

I always like to sit in the front row. The screen looks so big and the sound makes the seats vibrate. Mary Lou thought we should sit in the middle, halfway up. We had to climb all over a row of people to get to the seats she wanted. Then I remembered why I like to sit in the first row. You don't have to step on anybody to get to your seat.

As we were waiting for the movie to start, she told me how frustrated she was with her sister. It never seems to change. They just argue all the time and then she gets so upset that she cries and just wants to escape. I told her I know the feeling well.

I tried to help her get off the subject. She was so sad. I started goofing around, making jokes and funny sounds and stuff. Before I knew it she was smiling and laughing. That made me feel good. She was happy again, and then the movie started.

After the movie ended I walked her to the bottom of her street. We had a great time talking about the movie. I spun around mimicking Wall-E's movements and sounds and we both busted up over that. Heck, I look as round as him, so why not act like him?

When I'm with Mary Lou, time seems to fly. We were at her street before we knew it. She turned to me before she left and told me how much she enjoyed the movie and being with me. She told me it was one of the nicest times she had in awhile and she was happy she bumped into me today. She felt a lot better. And then it came out of the clear blue, caught me by surprise and knocked me off my feet; she put her hands on my shoulders and gave me a kiss.

My face must have turned a million shades of red. It was like a giant firecracker exploding inside my head. Wow! Awesome! Time stood still. I just stood there like a bowl of ice cream melting in the summer sun. I will never, ever, ever forget that moment.

Mary Lou told me thanks for a great afternoon and being a good friend. She turned around and walked up the hill. I was so happy. I just stood there for a few moments kinda shocked.

What a way to end the day. If only every day could be like this. Wouldn't it be a perfect life!

Journal Entry 20 – September 30

It paid off big today. I took a chance and it might have worked. I think I finally put a stop to Vinnie.

On Saturday our local high school was having its big grudge football game with the neighboring town's team. Every year, huge crowds from both towns pack the stands. Danny called me up and invited me to go with him and Tom to the game. I was excited that they still keep asking me along. I think they're pretty good friends.

It was an amazing game. Evil Vinnie was the quarterback today for our town's team, replacing the senior who injured his knee in the last game. Usually he's just a substitute and doesn't get to play much. Maybe that's part of why he's so mean—it's got to suck to be stuck on the sideline when you want to play. He thinks he's so tough and nobody can stop him, but he can't even get on the field. Maybe pounding on me makes him feel like a big shot again.

Today, though, he was the one who got pounded. Big time. I swear, it was my fantasy coming true. I couldn't believe my eyes. I'd imagined him getting crushed on a football field that day he beat me up with the Wiffle bat, and now it was happening. Wow!

On the very first play of the game Vinnie yelled out his numbers, took the snap, then got sacked by the linebacker of the other team. He went down HARD. I laughed so hard my stomach was aching. Wow! Double wow! Now he knows what it feels like, I thought.

Everyone around me looked at me, wondering why I was laughing at our quarterback getting slammed. Tom and Danny knew and kinda laughed with me. Danny said, "I told you he doesn't have an ounce of brains." I was almost sad when Vinnie got up and brushed it off.

But he wasn't up for long. Ha! On the second down, the ball was snapped and KA-BANG!, Vinnie went down a second time. They guy who crushed him was HUGE—and he just laid there on Vinnie for a while. It was hilarious! Still, Vinnie got up again and brushed off the grass. Gotta say, he did surprise me with that. I thought he'd be flattened like a pancake for good. He did look a little confused as he went back into the huddle, wobbling a little as he walked, but otherwise he was still functioning. From what I could make of the gestures he was making at his teammates, I figure he was telling them they need to protect him better. I didn't agree, of course.

The next couple of plays, Vinnie handed the ball off to his running back, escaping the wrath of the opposing team. It worked so they kept it up most of the game. Otherwise, every time Vinnie tried to throw the ball, he was knocked to the ground and buried by the big linemen on the other team. It was the best day of my life! I sat there completely happy. Vinnie was getting his. Maybe not from me, but that's fine, I've already lived the experience of slamming him during the game in my mind. And boy, did it feel GOOD.

Down after down, play after play, quarter after quarter, Vinnie got smacked down. Each time, he was slower about getting up and brushing it off. He started to stagger a little. One time he was even helped off the field by the medical team. Just like I'd imagined! Spooky.

Vinnie sat out for a couple of plays but came back near the end of the fourth quarter. I have to give him credit, continuing to come back after so many beatings. He sure could take it.

With thirty seconds on the play clock in the fourth quarter, the other team was ahead by seven and Vinnie was on their ten-yard line. All of us in the stands were on our feet, screaming and yelling and waving our arms. Vinnie was so close to tying the game. With the right play, we'd win. Part of me was rooting for Vinnie. I mean, if he pulled this off, my team would win. But most of me hoped that he'd get taken out for good. Call me evil for thinking that, but I couldn't help it. I'd never wish anyone else to get hurt, but Vinnie was different. Vinnie deserved it. It was only fair that he feel some of the pain he's dished out on me.

Even as I was thinking this, it's like there was no emotion inside of me—I was detached from the world. All business, baby. I didn't care that I was in a packed stadium, I didn't care that the players were screaming or that there was music playing. All I could see was Vinnie.

The ball was snapped and the opposing linebacker jumped over the tackles and flew into Vinnie—his shoulder buried deep into Vinnie's gut in the blink of an eye. Vinnie didn't see it coming. He'd just started to move backward. The force blew him ten yards back, with the linebacker embedded into him like a bullet. He landed HARD.

The game was over, but Vinnie wasn't getting back up. The medical team carried him off the field on a stretcher. I swear, it was just like my fantasy. Freaky! I didn't know what to think. I mean, I thought I'd feel great knowing he was hurt, but then I didn't feel so great after all. It's sort of like I made this happen. Yeah, sure, I know I can't just imagine something and then it happens, but still . . . a part of me felt guilty. The whole thing was crazy. Tom and Danny were sitting next to me saying, "He had it coming. Vinnie received his payback today." But for some reason all my happiness left, and now all I felt was terrible for sending someone to the hospital with my thoughts. How could I be so evil? I was no better than Vinnie.

Later in the day my dad was watching the news and told me that the high school football quarterback was in the hospital with a mild concussion. Doctors were expecting a full recovery. I felt like a ton of bricks had been lifted from my shoulders. At least I didn't kill Vinnie.

I can see the hospital from my upstairs bathroom window. It was weird, brushing my teeth and seeing the hospital and thinking about Vinnie lying in that building, all bandaged up. The same creepy feeling hit me the next morning when I was washing my face. But I couldn't <u>not</u> look over there. I couldn't shake the feeling that I put him there. Finally, I just felt so bad that I went downstairs, told my mom I was walking to the library, and then walked over to the hospital.

I found out what room Vinnie was in then sat in the lobby. What should I do now? Go up? Go home? Why did I even go there? After all, Vinnie has never, never been nice to me, so why should I be nice to him? What if I went up and he slapped me around and called me Yubbie and said mean things? Sometimes people get angrier when they're hurt. I got up to walk to the exit but then my feet turned to the elevator. Something inside of me was saying that this was the right thing to do.

I walked into his room and he was lying there with a bandage around his head. His eyes were closed and I thought I should just turn around and get out when all of a sudden his eyes opened. He said, "Yub...", and then he stopped. "I don't even know your real name," he finally said. I told him it was Joe and that I was at the game and saw what happened. I was in the area visiting an uncle at the hospital and thought I'd stop in to see if he was all right. He looked baffled.

He said, "Yeah, Joe, it was a tough game. A really tough game. But I'm okay." I didn't really know what else to say so I just said, "Good." Yeah, that seemed like what I needed to hear, that he was okay. I was ready to go home now. I turned to leave but he stopped me. "Hey," he said. He still looked confused. I mean, it is kind of weird that I would be there visiting him and all. But a good weird, in a way. "Thanks for stopping in, Joe," he said. And then he kind of smiled. It was a different smile than he ever showed me before. Usually, his smile was scary. This one was actually nice. I shrugged and kind of waved and then walked out.

Maybe I did something good today. I know I felt better inside knowing that he was okay and that the rest of my fantasy didn't come true. Maybe I learned a lesson about the way I think. Part of me wonders if we have power in our thought. The rest of me thinks the whole thing was just one big coincidence.

Journal Entry 21 - October 21

My miserable son of a beastonian father gave me a lickin' today that I'll never forget. My butt feels like I sat on a barbecue grill. I won't be able to sit for a week! I thought Vinnie's beating with the bat was bad, but the strap wins, hands down. I can't believe that my dad hits us so hard. My body feels like I went through a meat grinder.

It started a couple of days ago when Dad asked the three of us to do extra chores around the yard. Well, it wasn't asking. It was more like ordering us to work. It's not like we had a choice, but he agreed to give us extra money if we did a good job.

It was hard work, and in four hours we had the backyard

looking like the best lawns of the richest people in town. At least as good as the golf course, that's for sure. We thought we did a great job, and after we were done we asked Dad for the bonus money. Sounds fair enough, right?

Dad told us that he didn't have the money on him and he would give it to us the next day. No problem, I thought. I was really excited about having the cash to buy a couple of my favorite comic books. Usually my allowance doesn't give me enough after I buy my candy. Candy always wins out over a comic.

The next day when Dad came home from work we all ate supper. As nice as I could, I asked if we could get paid for the yard work. He practically bit my head off. "I just came home from a long day at work. Can't a man have peace and quiet?" Hey, he could have all the peace and quiet he wanted. All I wanted was my money.

Dad was in a totally sucky mood. He started arguing with Ma when she told him she needed to buy some things for the house and needed some dough. He went off the deep end, telling her that all he does is work—go to work, work hard all day, blah, blah blah. He said that after all that, he has to come home to a wife who is complaining about the hard-earned money he tries to make. He was really ticked, turning all red in the face and slamming his fork on his plate. Everybody kept quiet for the rest of the meal. We know better than to bug him, especially when he's in a miserable mood.

Today was Saturday. That usually means Dad's in a better mood since he doesn't have to go to work. Boy, was I wrong. The morning started off great, cleaning my room and taking care of my chores before I went down for lunch.

We were all at the kitchen table getting ready to eat when I thought it would be a good time to ask Dad for my money. I wanted to make sure the store didn't run out of the latest issues. As Ma was giving us lunch, I asked Dad for the money he owed me. Big mistake. I was polite about it, I swear! But he jumped up and grabbed me by the forearm and lifted me off the chair.

I started screaming. "I'm sorry, I'm sorry," over and over. He dragged me across the kitchen floor anyway. I tried to push back with my legs. It works well when I play football, but he's very strong and I couldn't resist his force. I knew what was going to happen and kept screaming, "Please, please, I'm sorry." It didn't matter. Dad was on a rampage, and I was his new victim. The monster was out of the box and wanted blood.

"I told you not to bug me about the money. You want the money? I'll give you the money. It's right in here!" He pulled me into the downstairs sewing room. By now he had the strap in his hand. I kept screaming, "Stop, please, stop. I won't ask again, I promise." But do you think he heard?

He hauled me into the room and slammed the door. Man, he was yelling loud. "You want your money, I'm gonna give you all you want right now. Take your pants down, take your pants down now!" I froze. No way did I want to undo my pants. My screaming wasn't working but that's all I could think of to do. "Don't hit me, please, please. Keep the money. I don't want it. Keep it!"

He still wasn't listening. He just whacked me with the strap, anyway. He kept hitting me—on my legs, on my butt, on my arms, even on my face. I swear, I thought he was going to kill me. My screams got louder and louder as his swings got harder and harder. I fell down and covered my head. His strap started hitting my back. The burn got worse after each blow. I finally just laid like a possum, playing dead, hoping he would stop. My face burned like someone had branded me with an iron.

Finally Ma came into the room and pleaded with Dad to stop. I thought he was going to hit her, too! But he didn't, he just told her to get out because he was going to teach me a lesson I'd never forget. She kept telling him that it was enough, but he kept hitting me. I've never seen him so angry. Never.

He finally stopped and told me to go to my room. I could barely get up, but I knew that I had no choice or he'd start bashing me again. I felt like someone had poured acid over every inch of me. But somehow I staggered up to my room. I could feel the welts on my legs rising up and making my muscles tight. It was so hard to walk. But I was still alive as I limped to my room. I was safe.

Downstairs my ma was yelling at Dad, telling him that I was just a little boy and there was no need to beat me like that. He told her to mind her business and know her place. He was the one who took care of the discipline, not her.

I still don't know why he got so mad. All I wanted was what I'd earned. I'll bet his boss doesn't beat him when he asks for his paycheck. Why did he beat me so hard? I hate him! It's bad enough I get picked on by kids and beat up by Vinnie. But even in my home I'm beat like some dog who just dumped on the rug or something. I hate him. I hate him so much! If I had a laser like they have in Star Wars, I'd seek out everyone—including my beastonian father!—who has ever hurt me and line them up at the interrogation chamber on the spacecraft and use the shock pulse of my laser to give them a feel of what they're doing to me. Take that, you evil being! I'd keep jolting them one after another with a blast until they were begging for mercy, and then I'd put it on destruct.

If this is what Ma calls love, I can't imagine what hate must be like.

I just wrote that, but then I remembered what happened to Vinnie. I imagined something bad would happen to him and then it did. I better stop thinking about my dad getting shot just in case there really is some power in my thought. After all, he's my dad.

I hate feeling this way. I hate hating people. It seems so wrong but I don't know what to do. My body hurts so much. My leg is swelling and the welts look like sunburn where I forgot to put on sunscreen. My cheek has a mark running from my ear to my chin. My back is stinging and my arms are glowing red from trying to block the strap. Why does Dad hate me so much? Why do I even want to live? I can't go on like this. I'm so alone, so scared, so desperate. I might not have to worry about jumping out the window—my dad will end my life for me.

Maybe I'll run away. Yeah. I'll pack my bags and slip out into the night. I know how to get out. I'll open my bedroom window and crawl out onto the roof of the porch. I'll jump off the roof into the bushes. I'll put myself in stealth mode. Nobody will even know I'm gone.

I'll run away to the ocean and jump on a freighter that'll take me to an island. It'll be a perfect island. The inhabitants will be kind. There will be no straps, no mean people, and everyone will accept me for who I am. They will be beautiful, happy people. They will treat me with love and help me build a large tree house.

They will give me food, and after a while I'll lose all my fat from eating coconuts and veggies. My skin will turn golden brown and all the red will fade away with my new tan. No more sunburns. It will be heavenly. There won't be any violence on the island—just love. Everything will be perfect. My life will change.

When I grow up someday I'll marry a beautiful island girl—maybe like Mary Lou. She'll be the perfect wife. She'll cook for me and take care of all my needs. We'll love each other and we'll never argue about money because you don't need money on this island. Everything is there for the taking and everyone will let you have anything they have.

I can see myself in my tree house having monkeys for pets. We can fish during the day and share our fish with the other inhabitants. I can grow a garden like Uncle Ozzie taught me. We can get running water to our tree house by using bamboo as a pipeline from the river. There will be beautiful, high waterfalls all over the island. We can go swimming in the fresh water ponds or take a tube down the river. We don't have to do anything we don't want to.

We don't have to do laundry, we don't have to go shopping, we don't have to go visiting boring relatives or listen to TV soaps. We'll have our own satellite TV and Internet. We'll have all the computer games we want with all the electricity we need. I'll use the waterfall to turn a large waterwheel and make electricity.

We don't have to worry about winter or snow or someone stealing my hat and throwing it up a telephone pole. There won't be telephone poles. We'll use drums to talk to the other inhabitants of the island. There won't be schools, either—just old people like the Indians had that pass on knowledge and information. There won't be report cards or detentions. It'll be perfect.

We can go sailing, swimming, snorkeling, and wind sailing whenever we want. No one can tell anyone what to do. No one will be able to beat me. There won't be any fighting. If anyone fights, they're fed to the sharks. If anyone hits, they'll be thrown in a cage with a vicious lion that eats them up.

I can be me. Everyone will love and respect me. My body will be cut, my hair will be long, and I'll live for a long time. Eventually I'll have children. I'll love my children. I'll tell them every day that I love them and that they are the most important part of my life. I'll cherish my children like they are gold treasures from the lost world of Atlantis. I won't ever yell at them, I won't ever hit them. I'll hug them every day. I'll give them anything they want and they won't have to do anything they don't want to do. If they misbehave, I'll still love them and hug them. I'll correct them with gentle talks. I'll make sure they never forget how important it is to love. They can have all the monkeys they want for pets and maybe even an iguana.

My children will learn all they need to know from me. The

most important lesson they have to learn is to love everyone and respect all people, no matter what they look like—if they are fat, skinny, or tall. All they have to do is just love everyone. It will be a perfect world.

Maybe like thinking about Vinnie getting slammed, if I think about this perfect island all the time, one day I'll find myself there. Wouldn't that be great? Perfect.

Journal Entry 22 - January 19

I just couldn't do it. I couldn't. Now I'm a total loser. What will the kids say at school tomorrow? I'll tell Ma that I don't feel good in the morning and stay home. She'll buy it.

Over the last couple of months I've kind of been bragging to the kids in my school about how awesome I am on the guitar. I even said I was thinking of starting a band. I know it's not true, but who does it hurt? It makes me feel important—like I'm somebody. The thing is, I didn't count on my school having a talent show. And I really didn't count on people wanting me to be in it.

The talent show was tonight, right after the Parent-Teacher Organization had their yearly dinner. My ma and dad never attend. I don't think they really care what I do in school. They would rather sit at home, watch TV, and have their drinks. They just can't be bothered with anything else. Whatever. I had to go because I had to work in the school cafeteria washing dishes. It's my new job. The cafeteria ladies offered me free lunches if I'd wash dishes at lunchtime. That means I can save my money for more candy. More candy? Bring it on! Besides, it's a lot of fun playing with the big washing machine. I get to rinse off the plates with this giant hose that's wound in a spring and bobbles like one of the bobble head dolls you see in the back of people's cars. It's cool! Then I get to put the plates in these tray containers and push them through this big machine that washes and dries them. It's easier than doing them at home, and I get paid. And tonight, I figured the job would get me out of the talent show.

The girl in charge of signing kids up for the show badgered me about it all week. I tried to explain to her that I had to work. She wouldn't accept no. She kept on insisting and insisting like a vulture pecking on a rotting carcass—she wouldn't give up. She told me she was going to put me on the list and would come and get me in the kitchen when it was time to perform. I told her no, but she walked off like a bird that got her fill and waddled off into the woods.

What was I supposed to do? I didn't want to get up in front of all those people and embarrass myself. I can't really play, never mind sing and play at the same time. I started plotting ways to get around it. A couple of days before the show, I came up with the bright idea of breaking my arm. I kept jumping off the walk in our backyard and slamming my forearm into the ground. I kept trying and trying, but it wouldn't break. Two days and hundreds of jumps later, my fat arm was sore but not broken.

The day of the show came and I hoped that Cathy had forgotten about me. I left my guitar at home just in case she remembered.

I was wrong on all fronts. Cathy must have a memory like an elephant. As I was washing the dishes in the washroom she comes in and says, "It's your time to get up on stage." I reminded her that I have to wash the dishes from the banquet, but she had that covered. "I talked to the ladies in the kitchen and they said you could take a break and come out and play," she said. Gee, thanks.

I put a sad look on my face and told her that darn, I didn't bring my guitar. She said, "That's okay. There are other kids with guitars and you can use one of theirs."

And I thought I was quick. "Well, their guitars might be tuned differently than mine, and it would be hard to sing if I'm in the wrong key." I thought it sounded good.

But Cathy was a shark smelling blood. She wouldn't give up. With each kick in the nose, she came back for another bite. Finally I told her that I had to go to the boy's room first before I got on stage. "Okay," she said as she walked away. I had a short break, but what was I supposed to do now? She expected me back. I felt like I had won, but now I needed a plan.

I hurried up and put the last tray of dishes in the washer, took off my apron, and went to the boys' room. I opened one of the stalls and climbed on top of the toilet, my feet on the seat so no one could see that anyone was in the stall.

I thought and thought, and then I waited and waited and waited until I figured everyone had left the hall. I felt awful. I know I make up stories that stretch the truth a little when I talk to kids, but they don't understand that I do it because ugly, fat, stupid people need to make stuff up so people won't hate them for being ugly, fat, and stupid. Now I feel like a big old wimp and a total loser. I ran away like a jackrabbit being chased by a hunting dog—right into its hole. I don't know which would be worse: feeling this way or having gone on stage and looked like an idiot. Neither is good, I think.

I spent an hour in that stall. It stank in there, but at least when I came out the hall was empty. I went back to the kitchen only to be spotted by one of the ladies. "What happened to you? You disappeared," she asked. I told her I'd had a bad stomach and sat on the toilet for the last hour. Nobody ever questions diarrhea. She looked kind of embarrassed and said maybe I'm getting a bug that was going around. I agreed, got my coat and hat, then left.

I sit here feeling mighty low. I'm a coward with a yellow stripe down my back—and cowards don't go on stage. Only super confident people who know they're good do stuff like that. How the heck do they get that confidence? Where does it come from? Maybe I can save up my money and buy some because I don't see it around me. If I had the money, I'd pay Jet Li to help me. He's not afraid of anything. Heck, in his movies he jumps off twenty-story buildings and lands on his feet. I've seen him jump right into a fire to save a girl in trouble. Jet Li isn't afraid to go on stage. And he's sure not afraid to play football in the park.

I can see it now. I'll bow to Jet Li as he presents me with the secret badge for courage after I demonstrate through my actions that I am brave. It's a special award for my attempt to save a girl stuck in a burning car that was ready to explode as the gas leaked from its tank.

The crowd gathered and everyone watched as the girl screamed for help. No one would do anything—like my new friends who didn't try to help me when Vinnie whacked me with that Wiffle bat. I'm riding my bike as I come up to the scene. I can't believe that everyone is just standing there while this girl is in danger of burning to death.

I drop my bike, run up to the burning car, and pull her out. Everyone is yelling, "Get back, get back. It's going to explode!" Everyone but me. I'm focused and determined. I can feel the heat from the burning car start to burn my clothing and melt my skin, but I know I can do this. I'm not afraid, even of dying, if I must.

I struggle and struggle 'cause her legs are trapped under the steering wheel. She says, "Go, go save yourself. I can't get out." "Joe doesn't wimp out!" I tell her. Then I spot a tire iron that fell out of her truck. I grab it, feeling the incredible pain of my skin burning. Even the strap takes second place to this intense pain. I use the tire iron as a lever and pry her loose.

She wraps her arms around my neck and I pull her from the car just in the nick of time. As I drag her away the entire car bursts into flames. Seconds separated her from death.

The ambulance arrives and she's put on a stretcher. They give her oxygen and she continues to hold my hand as though we were glued together. She pulls away the mask and asks me my name. "Thank you," she says. "Thank you so much for having the courage to face almost certain death to save my life. Everybody else was scared, and yet you risked your life. You are so brave." I humbly bow and say thank you. All in a day's work.

Journal Entry 23 - March 15

I'm not going to school tomorrow. No way. If I have to fake a cold, a stomachache, diarrhea, and a rash all at the same time to get my ma to let me stay home, then that's what I'll do. No way I'm going to school.

If it weren't for that stupid rainstorm we had yesterday, I wouldn't be in this mess. It flooded our school, which means my class had to go over to the old school that was waiting to be torn down. That place is a dump, but they don't have any other place to put us while they clean up the mud on the first floor of my school. They should've just cancelled school till it was cleaned up. But no, they had to go and threaten that we'd have to make up that time in summer. So there we were, in that broken-down building with broken-down stuff.

The classrooms were really different in the old days. They were big and had black boards surrounding two walls and had desks that didn't move. I couldn't believe it as I tried to sit behind a desk that was bolted to the floor. The chair was bolted to the floor, too. And that's what killed me.

I could barely get my fat stomach to fit between the desk and chair. When I sat down, my belly drooped on the desk. I had to suck it in to get it underneath. Wow, it was tight! Weren't there any fat kids in the old days? Maybe they didn't have enough food and everybody was skinny. Or maybe they were all farm kids who had to go to work every day, throwing bales of hay and bringing out buckets of water to the horses, and so they were thin.

Whatever, I was so squashed in there that I couldn't breathe naturally. If I let all my air out, then I felt like my back was pushing out the back of the chair, putting bad pressure on it. So I had to try not to breathe all the way out. Talk about impossible! Each time I did let air out, the back of the chair moved. All of a sudden there was a crack—a loud crack—like Paul Revere's shot that was heard around the world.

The back of the chair broke right off and I fell to the floor. Everyone in the room burst into hysterics. Even the teacher had to hold back her giggles as she made her way to help me. She said, "Are you all right, Joe?" but I know she was thinking, "That was the most hysterical thing EVER!"

Of course I wasn't all right. She just saw me crash to the floor! But you can't say stuff like that to a teacher, so instead I looked at her, smiled, and said, "Yeah, I'm fine. Must have been a defective chair. It's so old." I stuck my hand up looking for help to get up.

Despite my words, I'm mortified, embarrassed, humiliated, and ashamed. I still can't believe it happened. When I got up, I asked if I could be dismissed from the class. I didn't look at anybody, just at the floor. The teacher told me to go and see the school nurse.

The kids were still laughing as I made my way toward the door. I could hear comments coming from different kids like "the great whale has been beached" or "the blob has blooped on the floor" or "the great wall has collapsed."

I kept looking straight ahead and walked out. My teacher was telling the kids to knock it off as the door closed with a thud. Too little, too late, Teach. I really embarrassed myself this time. The hippo landed, put a dent in the earth, then waddled out of the classroom.

I have no idea how long the kids will razz me about this chair thing. It took almost a month for the gossip to die down about me hiding in the boys' room when it was my turn to get on stage. I never told anyone the truth about that night, so I don't know how they figured it out. Kids would constantly tease me about dropping my guitar pick down the toilet or hearing me practice while in the john. I tried not to let it bother me. No one knew the truth but me, so regardless of what they said, I didn't give any of them the satisfaction of knowing. I just told them that I had a job that night and it was to wash dishes, not play the guitar. If they wanted to hear me play, then they'd have to pay. Moola for music, folks.

But now this. What am I supposed to do this time? For sure I'm not going back to face these kids tomorrow. Impossible. Not gonna happen, even if I have to jump out the third floor window onto my head. After tomorrow, though, I just don't know. Maybe I can convince my parents to transfer me to another school, or maybe I can tell them that I really hurt my back and need to go to the hospital. People do it all the time. I hear about it on the news. They fake that they have an injury, go to the hospital, then sue the insurance company. Maybe that's what I should do.

Danny once told me that his dad, being a lawyer, gave him a book called "The Verdict." It talked exactly about that idea. People get into an accident but they don't get hurt as bad as they say. They sue the insurance company, get millions, and then run off to buy a big fancy house and never work again. After they leave the courthouse, they take off their braces and dance the Irish jig, bragging about how they beat the company out of millions.

It might just work. If I sued the school for the chair thing and got a couple of million dollars for my injuries, I could finally make Dad proud of me. To get his cut, he would have to promise never to hit me again and throw the strap away.

If he breaks the promise, he would have to give the money back. Ma will be happy 'cause she can buy things for the house and maybe she would stop drinking. I'll buy Randy a remote control boat, and I'll buy a new baseball glove and hat for Trevor. Everyone will be happy including me. I could take the extra money and get surgery to remove all my fat. Now that's an idea.

My world would be different. I would be slim and live in a large house with my own TV and X-box. I would have a movie theater in the basement with its own popcorn machine and butter dispenser. It would have a freezer with every kind of ice cream in the world, and I would only show movies that I like.

I would never have to go back to school. If I needed help, I would hire Danny's dad and he would take care of all my problems. What the heck, as long as you got money you don't need anybody, or at least that's what Dad says.

It's not hard for me to stretch the truth or exaggerate the facts, but I don't know if I could lie straight out when I was in court. They make you promise to tell the truth, so help ya. Anyways, it really sounds wrong to pretend that you're hurt when you're not and to take the money from some company.

I'm gonna have to think about this one.

Journal Entry 24 - May 10

Great night tonight! I was invited to Danny's house for supper. What a time I had! What a nice family. What a nice house. Wow! Everything that Danny has is so expensive. I wish his ma and dad could adopt me—life would be so much better.

Out of the blue I received a call from Danny inviting me to his house for supper. I'd never been there, but from the way Danny described it, I figured it was a mansion. They have all kinds of "collectables" as he called them—even pottery from the Ming Dynasty, whatever that is.

Danny said he and his dad would pick me up at the house. I felt funny having them come over. We live in an old house that needs a paint job. Ma complains to Dad about it and he keeps telling her that he'll buy the paint for her. I get the impression that if he buys the paint, she has to put it on the house because he has no intention of painting it himself.

Our house kinda sticks out because it needs so many repairs. But I didn't have a choice. Danny lives on the other side of town where all the rich people live. It was either have Dad bring me over or them pick me up. It's too far to walk at night. I don't like to ask Dad 'cause he complains about having to drag us around after a long day of work.

Danny lives in what he calls a gated community. He says you have to pass a large gate with a security guard to get on their street. I can see why his dad became a lawyer—lots of money.

Maybe I should hire him to sue the insurance company after falling off the chair at school. I only managed to fake out my ma for a couple of days after that happened, and then I had to go back and face the jokes in school, but I still limp whenever I remember to, just in case I do decide to sue for millions. I would agree to share the millions with Danny's dad. I thought I'd talk to him about it.

At six o'clock they arrived. I waited outside so they wouldn't have to knock on the door. I would die if they looked inside my house. All the rooms need paint and wall paper. The linoleum on some of the floors has holes, and there's a bit of a food smell when you come inside. The only thing we have of value is an old brass cigarette lighter that Dad says is an antique from the Navy. I don't know how much it's worth, but the fact that he won't even let us near it tells me it must be worth something.

Wow! What a car! Danny's dad drives a Mercedes Benz. Cool! It has leather everywhere inside. It has lights all over the place—even when you open the doors, the outside lights on the side come on. It's like a limo. I was so excited to have a ride in this fancy car. Once Danny told me that his car cost almost $100,000.00. That's close to a million.

There's a sound system with eight Bose speakers and an amplifier made special for the car. Danny put on some music and it sounded like you were at a concert. Well, like what I think a concert sounds like. I haven't actually been to one. Anyway, it was loud and clear.

The seats were so soft and the car smelled really good. It smelled like . . . well, very different from our old station wagon. The rear seat felt like a soft bed. When we go for a ride in Dad's car, it's like being squeezed into a sardine can. Randy and Trevor keep elbowing me 'cause they make me sit in the center.

Danny's dad said he was happy to see me again and happy to have me over for supper. He's way nice. On the way over we talked about the Scouts, and his dad even congratulated me on receiving the Scout of the Day award. He actually remembered that. When I'd told my dad, he'd said, "That's all you get? Some old patches? What kind of an award is that?"

Danny's dad always wants to know what I'm thinking or what I like to do. I feel special around him. He makes me think that I'm okay even if I am fat. Danny and Tom haven't ever called me Yubbie, and no one has ever said anything about my weight. I like them a lot.

Just like I imagined, Danny's house is a mansion. It's made out of brick and has large columns in the front like the southern plantation homes I saw in a book on the Civil War.

Man, I thought <u>we</u> had a yard to mow—Danny's yard looked like a golf course! He once told me that they have a gardener, a maid, and a company that comes in to mow their lawn and rake the leaves. Danny doesn't have to do any yard work. None. He gets an allowance and can buy almost anything he wants. More than once he's bought me a triple-decker stomach wrecker ice cream on a chocolate waffle cone, and that costs a lot of money.

Everything is so beautiful in his house. It all looks new and shiny. The floors are so shiny they look wet. I was afraid to walk normally 'cause I didn't want to slip and fall. Everywhere I look there's wood, including a huge staircase winding upstairs with paintings hanging on the wall. Every painting has a light above it so you can see it clearly. The house must be worth millions.

We sat down at the dining room table. It must have been fifty feet long. There were ten chairs around it with room to spare. I never saw so many forks, spoons, and knives. Far as I know, you only need one fork to eat. Weird.

They have this lady who brings out the food. Hot dogs and beans—my favorite! The lady carried the dogs out on a large silver platter. Then she brought out the beans in this huge bowl with fancy handles. I don't think this is what they normally eat, but when Danny asked me what my favorite food was, of course I said hot dogs and beans. I would've said boiled eggs on toast with crème sauce, but Ma told me that's an old Polish recipe and Danny isn't Polish.

Everything had been going perfectly. I asked if I could use the bathroom and Danny showed me to one they have downstairs. They have five bathrooms in this house. I was kinda shocked when I didn't see a shower or bathtub in this one. They must take baths and showers somewhere.

The bathroom, even without a place to bathe, was as big as our living room. Neat vases and things decorated the sink, shelves, and toilet. They had this bright white and blue pot, with all kinds of horses painted on it, sitting on top of the toilet tank. It was so pretty. I'd never seen anything like it. It looked really expensive. I picked it up to take a closer look when all of a sudden it slipped and fell through my hands, crashing into a thousand pieces on the tile floor.

Danny came to the door and said,"Are you alright, Joe?"

"Yup, everything's cool," I said. Liar!

What was I going to do? I didn't have any glue—like I could've glued it together if I did have some. It was totally smashed! If this was my house and I busted something, my dad would get the strap and give my butt a sunburn. What would Danny's dad do? I thought about hiding it behind the toilet and pretending that nothing ever happened. Then I thought about getting slick and telling them that it slid off the toilet when I sat down. Then I thought about climbing out of the bathroom window and running.

Only, I didn't want to lie or hide or have them think I was a liar. Danny and his dad have always been so nice to me. I came out of the bathroom and Danny was waiting to bring me back to the table."Danny, I got something terrible to tell ya," I said."When I was in the bathroom I picked up the thing on the toilet and it slipped from my hands and smashed on the floor. I'm so sorry. I'll try to buy you and your parents a new one."

He looked past me and saw the shattered pieces on the floor. Then he said, "It's okay, Joe, it was an accident." I wasn't quite sure how to take that, though. I mean, the vase was his parents', not his."Will your dad give me a beating for breaking it?" I asked. "Of course not. My dad has never hit me or anyone that I know." I was still suspicious, but he swore that was the truth. He told me that his dad "disciplines" him if he does something wrong or doesn't behave, but that usually means taking away a privilege he has or making him stay in his room. I couldn't believe it. No strap, no beatings. How can that be?

He told me to just be honest and everything would be okay.

Then he walked me to the dining room. I stood on the other side of the table from his dad, just in case I had to move quickly. That's worked for me before with Ma. Dad catches me no matter where I stand. Then I 'fessed up, talking faster than I probably needed to but I just wanted to get it over with. "Mr. Jones, when I went into your bathroom I picked up the blue vase on the toilet and I accidentally dropped it and I'm sorry, real sorry. I'll give you my allowance for the next year to pay for it. I'm real sorry." I tensed my muscles, totally ready to run. I figured if he jumped up from his chair to pop me, I had a direct beeline to the front door and I could be out of there before he even got around the table.

But I didn't need to run. "Commendable," he said. I stood like a goof, totally confused. Didn't he hear what I said?

I don't think I'll ever forget what he said after that. "Joe," he said, "you're an honest scout and that is commendable. It takes guts to be honest. I'm a lawyer and hear people lie everyday in court. It takes courage and bravery to be honest." I pinched myself on the wrist to make sure I was awake. How could this be? In my house the strap would have come flying off the wall. Mr. Jones was sitting there telling me "commendable." He wasn't yelling or swearing. Matter of fact, he didn't even look upset. I wondered what was wrong. Maybe he was going to sue me. Then I'd really be in trouble with Dad.

I was confused at his reaction. He explained that because I was willing to take responsibility, I didn't have to pay for the vase. He says people are always making excuses and blaming everybody else for stuff they do. I did the right thing, he said. I brought honor to the Boy Scouts by living their code of conduct. All I could think about was something I saw on a comedy TV show when a guy said, "Martha, I've died and gone to heaven." It must be, because I was still standing and no one was yelling. Danny's mother also said it was okay, that the vase could be replaced. All I had to do was clean it up, and Danny helped me do that. Then we got to have dessert. It was my favorite—pistachio cake with cream cheese frosting decorated with chocolate bits.

Danny's parents are so nice. He's so lucky. They are so good to me. Even after I broke something, they fed me my favorite dessert. Crazy!

After dessert we went to his room for a while and played some games. He has the latest and the fastest. He has it all. It's incredible.

Danny's dad took me home. We all talked about the upcoming events with the Boy Scouts, especially the weeklong Aquatic Course at Camp Eagle. They were happy that I planned to take part. Well, that's what I told them. I haven't asked Ma or Dad yet.

We finally arrived at my house. As I was getting out of the car, Danny's dad said something I never heard before in my life. He said, "Joe, I can tell good character in a person. Someday you are going to become someone very important. I don't know what, but I can sense something in you by the way you talk."

Who, me? Fat, stupid, ugly Yubbie, someone important? How can that be? Part of me wants to believe him. Heck, Danny's dad is smart and a lawyer and he sees something in me. Me. My dad keeps telling me that I won't add up to squat. He says I'll end up working next to him in the plant making roller chain. What does Danny's father know?

Maybe I'll become a mayor or even Governor. That would be cool. Then I'd get a house like Danny's and I'd have a limo take me wherever I want.

Why stop there? I can see it now: President Joe, the new leader of our country. Thousands of people will greet me as I land in my helicopter on the White House lawn. I'll walk off as the Marine guards salute me, and my little fuzzy dog will jump off and run behind me. I'll be someone important. I'll be the President of the United States!

Hmm. I wonder if you can be President if you have D's on your report card?

Journal Entry 25 - June 28

Magnifioso! Who would've thought I'd pass sixth grade! I just made it by the skin of my teeth. Maybe someday I'll do all my homework and get better grades. Ma and Dad never ask or say anything about homework, so why bother bringing it home? Now it's summer and I'm having a blast!

I couldn't believe it when Ma told me that I could go to the Aquatic Course at Camp Eagle. Knock me down with a feather, why don't you? I couldn't figure where they got the extra money to send me. I was told it cost a lot. Then Randy let it slip that Danny was behind it. Mr. Jones had called the Scout Master of our troop and suggested that Troop 56 sponsor one scout's expense to the Aquatic Course. It was also his idea that since I'd received the Scout of the Day award in last year's competition that I would be the scout to best represent the troop. Wow! Wow! Triple magnifioso. Wow! An all expense paid trip for me!

I still don't understand why Danny's father keeps on being so nice. Even after I broke the vase on his toilet! I asked Danny a couple of weeks after I broke it how much it cost to replace. He didn't really know but he said it had been in his family for many years and it couldn't be too bad. I felt horrible. Even after all that, Danny's father wants to be nice to me. I can't figure him out.

I don't look gift horses in the mouth, though, so here I am at Camp Eagle representing my troop. It's been a tough week. There are so many things I've had to do.

We have to swim every day and I love that part. I can still hold my breath underwater forever. We had to learn how to jump in the water and save someone from drowning. We even have to take the person and put our arm around them doing the sidestroke to bring them in. It's cool and I can do it. In the water, my blimp size body doesn't slow me down at all. Swimming is nothing like running and trying to jump over a log sawhorse.

We also learned how to row a boat, paddle a canoe, and start a gas engine on a boat. We even had to take the canoes out into the middle of the lake and tip them over. Most of us thought that was crazy. It's like jumping out of a perfectly good plane to parachute. We had to tip the canoe over and tip it upright again, getting all the water out, and then work as a team to get back in. That was the hard part.

I could easily tip it over and push on the bow (that's the front of the canoe) underwater while the stern (the back) pops out of the water and empties most of the water out. Getting back in is another matter. There were two of us in each canoe. After we emptied the water out, each of us would go to opposite sides of the middle of the canoe. One would rest his arms on the side while the other pushed his body out of the water and into the canoe. The leaders called that counterbalancing.

After the first guy gets in, he has to lean in the opposite direction of the other person. Then the guy in the water pushes himself out of the water and into the canoe, again counterbalancing the push. I make a perfect counterbalance. But when I tried to get in the canoe after my partner was in, I pushed down hard on the side and the canoe tipped over toward me, sending my partner flying into the water. For a split second I was totally embarrassed. But when he bobbed back up, he was laughing. So we both laughed. I don't think he was enough counterbalance for me.

We tried it a second time. That time I made the first attempt to get in. My partner tried to weigh down his side while I pushed up and really struggled to get my belly over the edge. I only made it up to my chest, leaving most of my body in the water. It took a few tries, but I finally wiggled my fat over the side and into the canoe. My body didn't fare so well. I have red marks going across my chest and stomach from the edge of the aluminum canoe. But I did it, and that's what matters!

I was happy. The water lets me compete with the other kids. Coming to an Aquatic Course was a good idea. There wasn't anything I couldn't do. Some of the kids made fun of me. I could hear them snickering in the background. But it was nowhere near as embarrassing as falling into the mud or getting hung up on the cargo net.

The week is almost over. Today we had to swim a mile, with the counselors in boats in the water, watching us swim. We all started out together. It was really tough. I tried hard to swim as fast as I could, and the burning started again in my arms and legs. "I can do it, I can do it," I repeated in my mind, like the day of the hike. It worked then, and it worked again today.

We could take breaks if we wanted, or change to easier strokes. After a while, I got really tired. I was kind of in the middle of the pack and that made me feel good. At least I wasn't the slowest. I changed to the breaststroke. I just kept telling myself, "I can do it, keep an even pace, stroke, burn, stroke, burn, stroke." I tried to ignore the burning.

After the halfway mark I was in the beginning of the pack.

When I realized that, I nearly drowned, then and there. There were only five or six scouts ahead of me! No one was going to make fun of me today. My heart was pounding and pounding. It got so loud that I could hear it in my ears. Between the burning and the pounding, my body was exhausted. I wasn't going to quit—no way! The little voice in my head kept saying, "You can do it, you can do it, just one more stroke."

I made it to shore. I was so happy! I wasn't the fastest, but I was number four out of twenty. Not bad for the fat kid! There were some scouts who didn't even make it and had to be brought into the boats, so I thought I did really good.

Something surprised me today. After the swim we all went to our campsites to change. There were scouts from troops all around the state. After we changed we went to the activity center. One of the scouts I met and was friendly with was Bobby. He told me he forgot his Scout hat at the campsite. We have to have it on when we're in the activity center.

He asked me if I wanted to walk back to the campsite with him. I agreed, and we asked permission. When he got to the site, no one was there. He went to his tent and came out with his hat. He told me he wanted to show me something and pulled a couple of cigarettes out of his pocket.

It didn't make sense. Here was a Scout and he smokes? That's bad. I know my mother smokes and coughs her head off all the time. But I never thought of trying a cigarette.

He offered me one but I said, "No, thanks." He said, "Come on, it ain't gonna kill ya. It's great." I looked to make sure there were no adults around. I knew I'd get in trouble. But the thing is, Bobby was my friend and one of the few scouts who would hang around with me. I couldn't say no—I might lose a friend at camp.

We sat by the fire and lit our cigarettes. As I inhaled my first time, I felt major pressure in my chest and started to cough like crazy. Bobby told me that was normal for a first time. It goes away after a while. I don't know about that. I kept smoking and kept choking. Everybody who smokes goes through this? My head started getting all dizzy and I thought I might heave. Woo! I told Bobby and he laughed. "You'll get used to it." He better be right.

When we finished we made sure that we hid the butts real good. Don't want to get caught! We headed down the path to the activity center. The woods were still spinning, and I was stumbling and tripping. Bobby was laughing and after a while I started to laugh, too. What the heck, there's no harm in having a good time. We weren't hurting anybody. He slipped me a couple of cigarettes and some matches just before we entered the activities center. I took them because I didn't want to offend him. I don't think I want to smoke again. I don't like being dizzy.

I'm almost ready to go to bed. I haven't felt right all day after smoking. Why would anyone want to smoke? It tastes terrible, makes you cough, gets you dizzy, and you want to puke. I'll throw the cigarettes away in the morning, as soon as I can sneak them into the trash.

I'll bet Olympic swimmers don't smoke. I could be like them. Mr. Jones said I'm supposed to be somebody important. Olympic gold medalist swimmers are important.

I can see it now. I'm on the staging board, slim and cut, wearing my Speedo. It's the final in the men's freestyle competition at the 2020 Olympics. The gun goes off and I jump in. The competition is fierce. The U.S. is tied with our archenemy, China, for the gold. My team is counting on me.

The swimmer from China and I are neck-and-neck in the first lap. As we take off for the last lap, I give it all I've got. My arms and legs start to burn, and all I can think is, "I can do it, I can do it, one more stroke." I keep pushing and pushing, burning and burning, but I know I can beat him.

I touch the wall before the guy from China. Before everybody! I did it. I won! And I set a new world record, too. Now I'm someone important!

Journal Entry 26 - July 15

I thought I came up with a really good plan for avoiding Vinnie at Anthony's Pool. I'd just swim at the Tofic River, instead. Clever, right? Wrong.

It wasn't the best plan from the beginning, I admit that. There are no pinball machines or video games, no pavilion, no rest rooms, no place to change, no soda and candy, no Mary Lou. But there's also no Vinnie. I don't know what happened to Vinnie after I saw him in the hospital. Maybe the good whack on his head made him meaner. I don't know and didn't want to take the chance of bumping into him. So it was me and the Tofic. And up until today, I thought I was all set.

The Tofic River has much colder water than Anthony's and is small, but it has its good parts. The cliffs around the natural basin are really high, maybe fifty or sixty feet. They're like the cliff you see in the high-diving competition in Hawaii every year. Well, maybe not that high. I don't have the guts to dive off the cliffs at Tofic, but I'll jump. Feet first isn't so scary.

Actually, jumping off the cliffs is really awesome. First you have to climb up the sheer cliffs, being very careful not to fall. Once you get to the ledge, you have to balance yourself on the rocks before you jump. Last year a kid dove off and hit his head on the bottom and split his skull. There are warning signs around, but nobody pays attention to them. Anyways, I figure that since I wear my sneakers when I'm jumping off, I'll be okay. Sneakers have good traction on the rocks.

There aren't a lot of kids hanging around the basin. I think the water is too cold for most people. I know if I stay in too long, my toes and feet turn purple. You have to jump in and get out right away to not freeze—and to get out of the way of the next jumper, if there is one. Today there wasn't anybody at the basin. The Boy Scouts have a buddy system and I know I'm violating the code, but it's hot and I wanted to swim. And it's not like I have buddies throwing themselves at my feet.

I made my first jump of the day and was coming out of the water when SPLASH! A big piece of sod and dirt hit the water right next to me, almost nailing me. I looked up to the top of the cliffs and there was Trevor with a bunch of his friends. They started throwing mud balls and sod patches at me, left and right. I was totally bombarded! I ducked underwater. Usually I can see pretty good under there—the water is crystal clear here—but everything was brown and dirty from all the mud they were throwing.

The mud bombs hit the water like the bullets, just like in that movie "Saving Private Ryan." I tried to keep underwater until I made the edge of the pool. When I got there I pulled myself up and tried to stand. BAM! BAM! BAM! I was totally peppered with mud wads. I was so mad. I couldn't use my towel because I had mud on my head, on my back, all over me. I screamed at Trevor as I dove into the water to wash off. Now it became a contest for him. I stayed in the water trying to dodge the mud balls. Every time I tried to get out, PLA-PLA-PLA!, I got hit. At least in the water they could only hit my head and I could drop down and rinse off.

They started calling me names like whale, hippo, and, of course, Yubbie. Trevor was challenging each of his buddies by saying you get ten points if you hit him in the head, fifteen if you hit him in his big belly. He was busting up the whole time. I swore I'd beat him up as soon as I could get out of the water.

Finally they stopped. Maybe they got tired or ran out of ammo, I didn't know. I waited for a couple of minutes before I tried to get out of the water. See, I know Trevor. He's tricky. He'd wait just long enough for me to towel dry and then PLA-PLA-PLA!

But even after I toweled off, no Trevor. They were gone. The whole way home, all I could think about was getting my hands on Trevor. I didn't care if it meant the strap. I'd give him a beating first and then get ready for mine.

When I got home Trevor was in the backyard. When he saw me, he busted up again. "What's the matter, Fatso? Get a little mud pie today?" he said. "You like to eat, Yubbie, so we thought we'd give you all the pie you could want." I ran after him, totally raging. But he can run fast, even faster backward than I can forward. He kept teasing me and teasing me. I finally said, "I'm gonna tell Ma and Dad. This time I didn't do nothing and you're gonna get the beating."

"Hold off, Blimp," he said. Then he told me he saw me going inside Ma's closet and going through her pocket books to steal money. That made me shut up and stop running after him. He threatened to tell. I wasn't so sure, but then he laid another bomb on me: He'd seen me smoking cigarettes at the basin before I climbed up the cliff to jump in.

That little snot! He's so sneaky. Now he's spying on me in the house! Of course I had to swipe a little cash from Ma—my allowance isn't enough to buy cigarettes. And I want them. Bobby was right. After the first time I didn't choke as much and it gave me a good feeling when I smoked. It helps me escape my troubles and relaxes me. I'm glad I forgot to throw out those cigarettes he gave me. When I found them in my pocket the next week, I thought, "What the heck?" and tried them and I liked it. I know it's bad, but so what? I'm fat and stupid, so it's right up my alley. What's the difference if I die from cancer? Nobody cares—especially not Trevor.

Trevor was smiling at me, the little twerp. He had me good and he knew it. Who cares that he does the same thing, picking Ma's pocketbook for loose change? I'll be the one who gets in trouble. I always am.

I took off my shirt tonight and I look like I was in a paintball shoot-out. My body is covered with polka dot bruises from the mud balls they were throwing. I hate Trevor.

One of these days I'll figure out a way to get Trevor. I know! I'll sneak into his bedroom in the middle of the night and pour honey over his entire body. Then I'll open up a giant crate of bees that I'd buy from a local farmer and let them loose. They'd attack the honey and keep on stinging and stinging him until it drives him mad. Maybe he'd run out of the house with the bees chasing him, trying to get to the river to jump into the water, and a black bear might jolt out of the woods and pounce on him to get the honey. I'd be laughing as he ran, and he would know I was watching him. Then he'd understand not to fool with me. He'd never be the same after that.

Journal Entry 27 - July 30

Why is it that as soon as I overcome one thing, another thing pops up?

After the river thing with Trevor, I decided to go back to Anthony's. I know Trevor. He's like a wild jackal. Once he sinks his teeth into his kill, he doesn't let go. I just knew he'd be back with his buddies throwing mud bombs at me if I tried to go to the river again. We both know I can't tell Ma or Dad 'cause he'll squeal. So, I'd just have to take my chances back at Anthony's.

This time I sat at a table near the main building so I'd be near the counter just in case Vinnie showed up with his boys. This way Mr. Anthony, the owner, might catch a glimpse of how he treats me and help me out.

I had called Mary Lou and told her I'd be there today. She's kind of afraid to go to the Tofic River because of the dangerous cliffs. She agreed to meet me at Anthony's.

We were sitting having a soda. I always sit facing the entrance after looking around the area to make sure I know who's there. This way I can see trouble coming in advance and have the time to escape. I'm trying to be smarter about this, I really am.

Just as expected, Vinnie and his boys cruised in the entrance. My body got all tense, my heart started pounding, and sweat beaded up on my forehead. I slowly got up from the table and walked towards the counter telling Mary Lou I was going to get a candy bar. She was facing me and didn't see the viper approaching.

I didn't want to run and cause attention. I should have. I didn't even make it to the counter before his henchmen cut me off from the opposite direction. One said, "Hey, Vinnie, look who's here violating your number one rule. Yubbie." I swallowed and tensed, waiting to be hit. To my shock, Vinnie said, "I don't have time for this. Let's get going. I don't have all day to waste."

Maybe something <u>did</u> happen that day at the hospital. Are my days of being screwed with over? Was my ounce of caring enough for him to leave me alone? I don't know if I can believe that, but I was truly happy that he didn't stop and bother me today.

I got my candy bar and went back to Mary Lou. By then she'd noticed Vinnie and his boys walking off to the pavilion. She told me to be careful 'cause she saw him when I went to the counter and that I'd just missed them. I mentioned how we crossed paths but Vinnie didn't say much today. Maybe he'd set his eyes on some other sucker. I felt relieved.

It was so awesome being able to just sit and talk to Mary Lou without worrying that I'm going to be flattened any minute. We spent a long time chatting and then decided to go for a swim. Worst decision of my day. We were standing next to the diving board, facing the pool, when all of a sudden someone yanked my swim trunks down from behind. And then I got shoved into the pool. It happened so fast I couldn't stop any of it.

I landed upside down in the water, totally struggling to regain control. I was gulping water all the way up to the top. But when I popped up, I realized my trunks had fallen off my ankles when I entered the water. I dove underwater, totally freaking out, to find my trunks. I mean, what if they weren't there? But they were—I spotted them sinking to the bottom and snatched them in the nick of time.

I came up looking for the culprit who did this to me. Vinnie, I figured. He'd faked me out, I was sure of it. Only it turned out not to be Vinnie. It was Trevor. He was standing by Mary Lou, laughing hysterically. His buddies were there, too. They'd followed me today to Anthony's. I was so embarrassed and mad. Everyone around the pool was laughing. Even Mary Lou was trying to hold her giggles back. What am I, a clown? Why does everyone always end up laughing at me? Well, not everyone.

The owner behind the counter saw what happened and came over and started yelling at Trevor and his friends to leave. Mr. Anthony told them he wouldn't tolerate that kind of behavior at his pool and if they didn't leave then he'd call the police. Trevor told Mr. Anthony not to touch him or he'd file a complaint against him. Then my wonderful little brother flipped me off. He took off with his buddies, acting like a big shot.

I couldn't believe what had happened. Everyone saw me naked and saw my privates. Everyone! Even Mary Lou. It's so wrong I can't even find the words for it. I should be the one calling the police on Trevor.

I got out of the pool with my bathing suit on and ran toward the lockers. Mr. Anthony tried to say something to me as I blasted past him, but who cared? He couldn't say anything to make this better. No one could. I put on my clothes and made a desperate dash to the exit. I tried not to look at all the kids still snickering and giggling. Mr.Anthony again tried to say something to me, but all I could think of doing was going home.

When I got home there was Trevor in the backyard waiting for me. He started in on me with all his "Hey, Yubbie, this," and "Hey, Yubbie, that." When he said, "Hey, Yubbie, show some of that elephant butt today? The whale lost his shorts and gave everyone a moon," I decided that he was finally going to get it. I started yelling at him, telling him that when he was asleep tonight I was going to come in and beat him up—real bad. I didn't even threaten telling my parents 'cause all he would do is blackmail me again for taking money from Ma's purse.

I turned around and started walking away when he jumped on my back and punched me in the head. I fell to the ground feeling pain in my eye. He jumped off me and said, "If you're gonna jump me in bed, then I'm gonna jump you first and get my hits in."

My eye burned and I ran to the house. Ma asked me why I was holding it, and I told her that Trevor had jumped on me and punched me. I could feel my eye swelling shut and it was hard to see. Ma looked at it and said, "Boy, you got a beauty. Put some ice on it." Ma went to the door and yelled at Trevor to get in the house. She asked him why he punched me. He told her I won't leave him alone and kept picking on him. I couldn't believe his lies.

She told him to go to his room and when Dad came home he would deal with it. She tried to slap him when he walked by her, but Trevor's fast and he ducked out of the way in time. She told me to go lay down on the couch and keep the ice on my eye.

When Dad got home, Ma told him what happened as soon as he walked in the door. He slammed the door shut and didn't even take off his hat. He grabbed the strap and came into the den towards me. I started shivering thinking I was gonna get a beatin' because I had the swollen eye. He said, "Let me see." I pulled off the ice pack. He did even speak a word. His face turned beet red, and he turned around and went flying upstairs.

I could hear Trevor wailing in pain. They were screams of pain like you hear in the torture chambers in the medieval times. Whew!! He was getting his. Better than I could've served up by jumping him in the middle of the night, that's for sure. It sounded like a wounded animal getting ready to die.

I was happy to hear his pain. He deserved every bit of it. Why should I feel bad for him? He should suffer at the hands of the Torture Chamber Master. Maybe Dad would put him in one of those iron cages with the spikes. When you close the door, the steel spikes pierce your body. Or the blood chamber that Blade was put in by his archenemy to get his special powers. Maybe the Torture Master would put Trevor on the rack and stretch him a couple of feet, or hang him by his feet into the pit filled with snakes and piranha fish. It sounded like the jackal was getting torn apart by a lion. Trevor was going to hurt for a while. No doubt about that.

The screaming stopped and I heard Dad coming downstairs. I held my breath and tensed, thinking I might not escape the Torture Master's wrath. He came into the room breathing fire from his nose, drool dripping from his fangs. His blood-shot eyes were bulging out like a beast whose appetite wasn't satisfied. He looked at me and said, "If you guys don't stop fighting, next time you're gonna get worse than a black eye from me." I didn't move an inch, frozen like a possum trying to avoid being eaten by the grizzly.

Trevor hasn't come out of his room. I'm not sure if he's even alive in there. When I got ready for bed a few minutes ago, I looked at my face. Now not only am I fat, I'm also very ugly. My face is black and blue and my eye is swollen shut. Looks like Rocky Balboa took a shot at me. I wonder how long it'll take to look human again?

Maybe being an alien would be better. I could be a Martian living on Mars—anywhere but here. There must be a way to escape from the Castle of Evil like they did in Narnia. Maybe there's a hidden tunnel in the basement, or a closet that leads to another world—one very far away from the torture chamber. A place where the animals can talk to you, enjoy your company, and invite you into their tree trunk for supper.

I know that if I was there, I would finally have the dog I always wanted—a trusty German Sheppard called Fritz. Fritz and I would make friends with all the animals of the forest and hide from the Torture Master. The animals would let us use their underground home to avoid the wrath of the whip. We would be happy, and all the animals would love me.

Journal Entry 28 - August 15

It worked! The Torture Chamber Master's attitude adjuster has disappeared forever, never to surface again from the dark regions of Dad's Dungeon! I'm the one who made it disappear—and I actually lived to tell about it. Wild!

It all started today when I decided to sneak my BB gun out and take it into the woods. Ma and Dad never let me carry it out of the yard. I don't know why, but they don't. It gets boring just plinking around at a cardboard box with soda caps! I can now take 50 paces and hit one cap after another. One shot—one cap. I need something more.

So I decided to take it out to the woods and see what I could do. I figured I could probably hit a bird at a hundred yards. That would be so cool! Just call me Davy Crockett! The guy could hit a deer at a mile away with his trusty gun. He probably had a nickname for his rifle, like Old Betsy. All the really cool gunslingers name their weapons.

My trick was to sneak the BB gun out my bedroom window. The plan was to set the gun on the roof of the porch, an easy place for me to reach once I left the house. But as I ducked out of my window to place my BB gun, stupid Trevor walked past my door and spotted me. I had to tell him what I was up to. I mean, he'd run straight down to Ma if I didn't. Maybe there'd be a chance he'd think it was cool and not tell? Keep dreaming, Joe. Oh, the little rat fink Trevor did think it was cool—but he wanted to go with me! He said I had to take him with me or he'd tell. I hate that kid. But of course, I took him. I kind of figured that maybe when we were out in the woods I could threaten to shoot him if he doesn't stop picking on me. Or maybe somehow shooting together would make us better friends. The best gunslingers always learned to respect each other over the barrel of a gun, right? Either way, maybe this was a chance to get Trevor to lay off.

After lunch, we told Ma we were going to the river for the afternoon. Neither of us knew that Ma heard us trying to retrieve the BB gun off the roof when we were standing on the porch railing making all kinds of noise to reach it. The column from the rail of the porch to the roof was taller than both of us. We kept trying to jump up and grab the barrel that was sticking out over the edge of the roof. It was kind of fun, I have to admit. But Ma was in the storage room and heard it all.

Trevor finally got hold of the gun and brought it down. That's when Ma came busting through the door, yelling at us. But she's way too slow. We booked out of there and were gone for the afternoon.

It's weird, I know, but Trevor and I had an awesome time in the woods. He still called me Yubbie, but I'm so used to it by now that I barely noticed. We walked around for hours taking pot shots at the birds in the trees. It was way harder than hitting soda caps. Sometimes a bird would land on a branch, and by the time we cocked the barrel the bird would fly off again. No way could we hit a bird in flight. I'll bet Davy Crockett could.

It was getting late and we decided to go home. We had to get the BB gun on top of the roof before we entered the house. Since Trevor was the only one of us who could jump high enough, he decided to make the first attempt. We totally forgot about Ma.

As Trevor climbed up on the railing, the door opened and there was Ma. Uh oh! We were snagged! She tore out of there, yelling at the top of her lungs. I nearly dropped flat to the ground and covered my head when she grabbed the BB gun from Trevor's hand and threw it on the floor. Doesn't she know not to throw a loaded BB gun? Maybe she didn't care, though, 'cause she was really ticked. She started trying to slap me. As usual, I made the mistake of trying to protect myself from her swinging arms by putting my forearm in front of my face, which meant she hit my forearm with hers. That really flipped her out. "That's going to be a bruise, I know it!" She shouted.

Ma for some reason bruises real easy. Maybe because of her drinking, I don't know. But she does. Hearing her screaming about a bruise, Trevor and I both knew what she was going to say next: "Wait till your father gets home and I tell him what you two did. Now I'm going to have a bruise from you hitting me."

Not good and we both knew it. We were in the same boat—and it was going <u>down</u>. Dad would beat the crap out of us in about two hours. Trevor dangled off the railing then dropped down. We each could sense the other's fear as the color left our faces. We were dead. It was time to go to the executioner. The Torture Chamber Master would have a field day on us. He'd take out his attitude adjuster and light it on fire. It was going to burn, burn, and burn. Maybe he'd have mercy on both of us and just put us in front of a firing line? Being shot in the head and dying has to be less painful that welts on our bodies that burn for days.

Ma told us to go to our rooms. She took the BB gun into the house and held the door as we both ran upstairs to wait for our punishment. Sometimes I don't know what's worse, the actual beating or waiting for Dad to come home knowing I'm about to meet the Torture Chamber Master.

Now that both of us were in a fix, we plotted our next move. We talked about going out my bedroom window onto the porch and jumping the two stories, hoping we'd survive the fall. Trevor had a better chance at that than me. Then we'd run away.

Or maybe we could go up into the attic and hide in the crawl space for several days. Maybe Dad would forget about beating us. Yeah, right.

Then we came up with the perfect idea. We could hide the Torture Master's whip, the strap. Without his whip what could he do—slap us? I'd take that over welts on my body any day. But how would we trick Ma as we snatched the strap? It hung on the kitchen wall, which was pretty much her domain. Dad said it hung there as a reminder of good behavior. And getting it was only half the problem. Once we had it, what would we do with it?

Knowing our execution was coming soon, our minds were working overtime. We came up with the plan. I'd go out the window of my bedroom, lay down on the porch roof, and throw one of my toys or old sneakers at the front door to make a sound like someone on the porch. Ma would go check on the ruckus. That's when Trevor would quietly run downstairs, snatch the strap, and hide it somewhere. But where? Trevor finally came up with that idea: We'd hide it in the oven. The perfect place! Why would they look in the oven? Ma hasn't cooked lately, so that would be the last place anyone would look. Maybe after they spent enough time looking for the Torture Master's whip, he'd run out of energy and not have enough to give us a good beating. It sounded like a plan. What did we have to lose? We were dead meat if we didn't do anything. That we knew for sure.

The plan worked out perfectly. Hearing the sound, Ma went to the front door as Trevor made it downstairs on the opposite side of the house. He took the strap and threw it quietly into the oven then ran back upstairs.

Ma returned to the kitchen, never realizing she'd been duped. I can just imagine her standing at the front door, looking all confused. Score one for the kids! Trevor, my archenemy, was now my comrade at arms. It was weird, sitting in my bedroom with him bragging about what we just pulled off. We put one over on Ma and Dad, and we'd receive a pardon for our efforts. What a relief.

What we didn't count on was that Ma planned on baking a roast for supper and had to preheat the oven. Fifteen minutes later, black smoke was spewing from the oven. The smoke detector in the kitchen went off. I thought for sure I'd go deaf! Those things are loud.

We ran downstairs not knowing what happened, thinking maybe there was a fire in the basement. The second we saw the black smoke in the kitchen, we knew what it was from. The whip had been cooked like a turkey on Thanksgiving, and it wasn't going to create any more problems in our lives. I did a happy dance right there in the kitchen doorway.

Ma quickly shut off the oven, pulled the rack out with the melting rubber-leather, and ran it outside, throwing it on the driveway. I stopped dancing. We swallowed hard. Now what was going to happen? We both ran upstairs and into my bedroom awaiting our fate. Ma screamed at us. "Wait till your dad comes home!" Yikes! Double and triple yikes! We were still gonna get it. Maybe we should've gone with plan A, the run away plan. But it was too late now—we could hear Dad's car drive in the driveway.

The Torture Master was home.

We heard the back door of the house close and Ma talking. Then everything went silent. Trevor tiptoed back into his bedroom. The Torture Master was devising a plan below in the dungeon. Maybe he was going to send up his henchmen to put us in chains and throw us on the rack.

I couldn't believe what happened next. Nothing! Absolutely nothing! The rear door slammed closed again and that was it. Was the Torture Master retreating after his torture session had been robbed from him? Or was he going out to the shed to create another device?

Trevor whispered down the hall to me. I went into his room. It overlooked the shed. Dad was there, holding my BB gun. Trevor grabbed at my arm, total terror on his face. He was probably thinking the same thing I was: Dad was going to shoot us. But then, in one big swoop like Babe Ruth getting ready to hit a grand slam, he wound up his swing using the gun as the bat and let loose, producing a piercing crack as it hit the shed. It splintered in a million pieces, the only part left was the barrel that he held in his hand.

Then the Torture Master turned and looked up at us in Trevor's window. We both ducked down. We didn't know if he saw us or not. A sinking feeling came over me. What was going to happen next?

Again the rear door slammed shut, and again dead silence. I tiptoed back to my room waiting for the attack to unfold. How do you prepare? What can you do when you know you're going to get the beating of your life? You sweat and pray.

I sweated and prayed a long time. I didn't hear a sound from downstairs until the TV went on. How could this be? Was the Torture Master waiting for us to go to sleep so he could finish us off then? Would he cover our heads with our blankets and remove us from the house? He could take us to the shed, his second dungeon, and tie us up and beat us with the BB gun barrel.

I'm going to bed soon with no idea what's coming next. Maybe if he opens my door and sees me sleeping innocently he'll show mercy and not pulverize me. Or maybe he'll do nothing? Maybe we really did pull one over on him this time?

I can see it now. The knight in shining armor has outmaneuvered the villain. The Torture Master has met his match and is confused knowing that the knight has spoiled his evil plans. The knight may have lost one of his swords in the plot, but the Torture Chamber Master has lost his magical whip—never to raise havoc again. The shining knight has saved the empire and the people are free to live in peace again. Cool!

Journal Entry 29 - August 29

Mary Lou has to leave town with her family. Her dad got something called a transfer and they have to move to another town almost across the whole country. I'm losing the only girl who wants anything to do with me.

There are a lot of other girls I'd like to get to know, but I can tell they'd only reject me. They are all really pretty and go out with boys that are skinny. What kind of a chance do I have against those other boys?

I try to impress kids with my long stories about how I took on ten other kids who tried to beat me up and put two of them in the hospital and the other ones ran away after seeing their buddies' punches bounce off my belly. Or stories about me taking a running start and flattening the bad kids like pancakes against the wall. I think they believe me. I try to make them laugh so they'll like me. The girls have really never been too mean to me. Well, there were a couple who called me "blimp" and "porker," but those were just mean girls.

Most girls are polite to me, but I'm afraid to ask them to go to the movies with me or take a walk and talk. I don't want to be rejected. It makes me feel awful. I try to talk myself into asking, but when the moment of truth comes, I chicken out. I hate that feeling, too. Either way, I feel like a dork. I'm fat, ugly, and stupid, and that's the truth. Why would any girl go out with me?

Mary Lou was the only girl that understood me. And now she's moving away.

Maybe I should just run off and become a monk like David Carradine when he played Caine in "Kung Fu." He doesn't have to worry about asking girls for a date. Monks can't go out on dates because they're always practicing Kung Fu and sitting in front of burning incense going "Ohmmmm." It doesn't sound like a lot of fun, but they don't seem to worry about girls. I never thought of that!

It's hard for me 'cause I hate the thought of a girl telling me no. Trevor, though, he has all the girls he wants. Everywhere he goes, girls flock to him like bees to honey. He's thin and in good shape. He has dark skin and dark hair—maybe that's what the girls like. He's still in fifth grade so he has girlfriends but he hasn't really started "dating" them yet. I'm blonde with very pale skin—and fat, of course. Girls seem to like fat only if I'm a clown.

If they ever knew how much of a slob Trevor is they would never even want to talk to him. He throws his dirty underwear under his bed and doesn't like to take baths. Ma says he has some kind of a problem because his T-shirts turn yellow in his armpits from his sweat and he stinks. When you walk into his bedroom, it stinks. I think he's the one who makes the whole house stink. I'll bet the girls would change their minds about him in a heartbeat if they knew.

Now I'm going to lose the only girl who ever wanted me. I could always tell just by the way she would look at me. I could see in her eyes we had a connection. I don't get the same feeling from any other girls. She's nice and always pretty happy.

We kept talking to each other at school and would go to different places to talk. I always tried to make her laugh. She keeps telling me I should become a professional comedian like Eddie Murphy. I don't know what she sees in me. She tells me that she thinks I'm a kind person and very sensitive, not only to the feelings of others, but sensitive about other kids picking on me. She's sure right about feeling terrible when kids pick on me.

Maybe I'll run away and go out west to live with Mary Lou and her family. From the way she talks, her dad doesn't beat her with a belt or strap. Me and Trevor didn't get in any more trouble that night after we fried Dad's strap, but we were surprised the next day. He invented something new.

The next day, the Torture Chamber Master came home after work and gave us a first-hand education with his new diabolical torture device—his belt. Now he didn't need to run to the kitchen wall to get his attitude adjuster—he wore it on his hips like a gunslinger ready to jump into action at the drop of a hat.

Now the welts weren't as wide but the burn was the same. I don't think Dad would like it if we put his belts in the oven and cooked them. But it's an idea.

I don't know what I could do to have Mary Lou's dad adopt me and take me with them. I'd probably have to get a job and support myself. I now make $20.00 a week washing dishes in the cafeteria. I wonder how much I'd need to take care of myself? If Dad didn't break my BB gun, I could do what Davy Crockett did. I read up on his life on the Internet. He ran away from home when he was real young, and he had his gun with him. His dad also beat up on him. The story goes that Davy beat up a bully at school who was calling him mean names on the first day and he tried to avoid the teacher's whipping stick by skipping class. After a while the teacher decided to write his dad a letter wondering why Davy wasn't coming to school. His dad got really mad. Davy knew he'd get one serious whoopin' so he ran away from home and lived in the woods for a couple of years. I think he was about my age when he left because it said he returned home at fifteen, three years after he took off. I could do that.

I wonder if with all my Boy Scout training I could survive in the woods around the Tofic River. I know no one would ever find me. I know where to hide, like Indian Rock and Big basin. There are caves all over the place. No one could find me if I didn't want them to.

The only problem is, I don't have a BB gun anymore. Maybe it doesn't matter. I'd probably need a rifle like Davy, anyway, so that I could shoot deer and rabbit for food. Dad has a bunch of rifles in his cabinet, but he'd freak if I touched those. The other problem is, Dad keeps the rifles locked up. Oh, well.

Maybe I should just get another job and make a whole bunch of money. The girls would like me then. I see it on TV all the time. I can see myself now, riding in a limo with two hot girls on each side of me, all of us drinking the bubbly stuff. The limo stops in front of my club and the driver opens the door. We all get out and walk down the red carpet. I have a fur coat with a fur hat like Denzel Washington did in "American Gangster." I strut down the red carpet while all the girls on the side call out my name, wanting to be part of my harem. We get up to the dressing room and there's Trevor behind the counter taking coats. My glamorous girls give him their coats without a second glance. Why? Because they're focusing on me.

Journal Entry 30 - September 10

Wow! I'm excited to start seventh grade, being with all the big kids at junior high. Middle school was pretty tough, but I passed sixth grade. I'm having a hard time with schoolwork.

I still haven't taken any home. I try to finish everything at school during study period, and if I don't, I don't. Ma and Dad couldn't care less how we do in school or if we bring anything home. Here's where I have it better than Danny. He has to bring schoolwork home every day and study for at least an hour. Suck city! He's missing all the after school cartoons, and the only chance he has to get out of the house during the week is Boy Scouts, his chess club, or his reading club. I can't even imagine having a club to read books. It's bad enough we have to read them in school. But to then join a club and go to a meeting to discuss the book you read? Ain't gonna happen.

Belonging to his reading club might have helped me today. I don't understand my English teacher. Yesterday when we got into class she gave us a project. She put on some classical music and told us to write our impressions of what we were hearing. Seemed kind of weird to me, but I tried.

This English teacher is called Porky. She has a face like a pig. I know it's mean, but she does. She's also fat like me. She waddles around the classroom like a pig going to the trough. I heard from some of the older kids that she falls asleep at her desk during class. She has one foot on the bottom drawer of her desk and leans back in her chair to fall asleep. The kids really make fun of her. Will that be me in the future—some fat slob taking snoozes during the day after I eat a big lunch? I couldn't get this picture out of my head, so I weighed myself when I got home. It said 210 pounds. I think I'm well on my way.

Anyway, I sat there and listened and listened to the music, but nothing really came to mind. I still don't understood what she wanted. What does the music sound like to me? What a lame question! But I had to write something so I thought and thought and finally started to write. To me, the music sounded like a locomotive on the track chugging long. Sometimes it sounded like it was trying to go up a mountain and other times it was going down.

I could sit back and see it. Just like out of the Wild West. Or like Jim West in the "Wild, Wild West," in his fancy locomotive with Artemus Gordon. What a neat train. They have a pool table that flips upside down as an escape hatch. They have all kinds of cool gadgets, and they try to get Dr. Loveless. It's a fun old TV series that I get to see sometimes late at night.

As I listened to the music, I started to write like I was in the train looking outside and seeing all the cacti and desert animals. It was a fantastic ride going through the Black Hills, the Bad Lands of South Dakota. I imagined Dr. Loveless chasing us with his spider-like contraption as our train rushed toward Mount Rushmore. I was trying to stop the evil doctor from defacing the Presidents with his jackhammer legs. We sped through the mountains and into the valleys trying to catch up with him. The engine was whining and the horn blowing as the landscape passed by the window.

We finally slowed down as the people in the area brought out the local marching band to play for us. You could hear the drummers drumming their drums and the trumpets blasting in the air, with flutes and all kinds of other instruments blaring, too.

I thought I did really well. I wrote just exactly what I thought I heard. I walked out of class thinking I aced this paper. What an awesome start to seventh grade English!

I couldn't believe my eyes when I got back my paper today. I got an F. An F! She also made a note on my paper: "How could you have ever heard this? Impossible. Ridiculous." What is she talking about, saying it's impossible? She asked what I heard and that's what I heard. How could it be impossible? How could it be ridiculous? It was my opinion, not hers. I heard what I heard, and I got an F for hearing what I heard and not hearing what she wanted me to hear. If I knew what she wanted me to hear I would have written about what she wanted me to hear. I feel stupid. Maybe there's something wrong with my brain.

Maybe there's nothing wrong with my brain. Maybe it's my ears that are on the fritz. Maybe I have fat deposits inside my ears that don't let me hear what other people hear and that's why I heard all the wrong stuff. It's not fair, though—just because what I heard wasn't what I was supposed to hear, I flunked. What a sucky deal.

Well, I might end up as fat but I know I ain't going to be a teacher. I mean, how would I be able to teach the students if I can't hear right? They might be asking a question, but I might be thinking they're giving me an answer. That would be very confusing. They'd also probably come up with a name for me.

Instead of calling me Yubbie, they might call me the "deaf pig" or "porky with stuffed ears" or "fatso with wax in his ears." I don't think I could take that.

Why can't I do anything right? I'm just downright stupid and fat, that's why. I should have Dad check to see if the scale is working—210 pounds doesn't seem right. They'll probably ship me out to the lame fat farm for kids who are stupid and fat. An F? It's garbage—all a bunch of garbage.

I'll show them all one day when I get the Pulitzer Prize for Genius. Maybe lightening will strike me in the head and I'll become a genius just like the movie I watched. I can see it now. Zap! I wake up and all of a sudden I'm doing mathematical formulas that even the teachers can't do.

The President of the United States will summon me to the White House. We're in crisis, he'll tell me. There's a meteor coming straight toward earth and it'll devastate the planet unless somebody can come up with the right mathematical answer to the equation needed to determine how many and how big the missiles have to be to hit the meteor and save the day. It's tricky because you have to take into consideration trajectory, speed, wind, and gravity. I'm the only genius on the planet who can figure it out accurately. I don't even need a computer. I can figure it out in my head.

I'm down in the basement of the White House in the command center. The President greets me and thanks me for taking time out of my busy day to come to his assistance. Frantic, he pleads with me to find the answer that all the computers and all the smart people of the world haven't been able to come up with.

I pat him on the shoulder. "No problem, Mr. President. Piece of cake." I study the problem and in minutes I call him back over and give him the answer. He instructs all the brilliant scientists at the command center to implement my directions. They don't agree. They say, "It's impossible! It's ridiculous!" The President looks at me and I nod my head with confidence. He tells them, "Do it. I order you to do it now!" Shaking their heads, they put in the answer and the missiles go off at their target. The rockets hit the meteor perfectly and it explodes into a zillion pieces coming down and burning up in the atmosphere.

I'm the hero of the day. I look at all the scientists who doubted my decision and say, "Impossible? Ridiculous? Show's what you know." The President comes over to me and hugs me then invites me to supper with the First Lady. They're having my favorite tonight, boiled eggs over toast with a special cream sauce. Perfect.

Journal Entry 31 - September 29

Ba da boom! I got my first real job. I can't believe it. I started today. Wowser, wowser, wowser!

I decided to look for a real part-time job once I started seventh grade. I don't get enough allowance and if I ever want to buy a real guitar, dog, or weights, I'm gonna have to do it myself. Ma and Dad sure ain't gonna help.

I talked to Danny last week and told him I need to earn some money and asked if he knew anyone looking to hire a thirteen-year-old. He called me back a couple of days later and told me that he talked to Tom. Tom asked his father, who is an accountant, if he had any clients who need extra help. It was good timing, because one of his clients was in the office a week ago and asked Tom's father if Tom would like a part-time job after school. Mr. Hurley is the guy's name. He owns a store and was looking for a stock boy. Tom's dad didn't think Tom had the time to work since he plays three sports in school and is in the honor society. Perfect for me!

Danny gave me Mr. Hurley's address and told me to use

Tom's dad's name when I went down to the store. It's called the Columbia Cash Market. It's on Columbia Street, a forty-minute walk from my house. I went down today after school to talk to him.

Mr. Hurley is very different looking. He's bald-headed and has a large white mustache. He looks like a miniature Hulk with muscles bulging out of his shirt. He looked very mean when I first walked into the store and I almost turned around and left. In a very deep, rough voice he asked me how he could help me. Not what I expected! I was bracing for, "What do you want, fat kid?" or something like that. Thing is, he turned out to be a really nice guy. He told me that he and his two brothers own the grocery store. It's been in their family for fifty years. Their dad started the store, and the three sons continued to work and own the store after their dad died.

Mr. Hurley told me to call him Max. It's not his real name. It's a nickname he picked up when he was in the Middle East fighting with the 101st Airborne. He told me it was short for Mad Max because he did a lot of things when he was fighting in Desert Storm that people thought were crazy. I kind of want to know more about that, but he really didn't get into it.

The job is three days a week from 3:00 to 6:00 PM and Saturday 8:00 AM to 5:00 PM. It pays $125.00 a week. Did I strike the lottery or what?! Max says I have to stock shelves and clean up during the week and make deliveries with him on Saturday afternoons. I also have to clean his station wagon and the meat cutting machines on Saturday before I leave. Piece of cake.

Max said that if I had the time, I should stay that afternoon and help out, kind of like a try out, I guess. I called Ma. She said that was okay and to be home by 6:30 PM. I didn't think she'd mind. If I have a job, that means she won't have to give me an allowance anymore. She cut off Randy when he started working in the Stop & Shop when he was sixteen.

It was an easy job. Max showed me how to change the prices on the marking tool and let me start putting up the stock in the store. I liked it. After I filled the shelves, Max told me I had to put all the remaining stock down in the cellar below.

Next I had to clean up and sweep the floor before I could go. I was sweeping around the cash register and found some change on the floor. I thought for a minute that I could just put it in my pocket and nobody would know the difference. It was just a few cents. But then I thought of what Danny's father said to me the day I broke the vase: "Honesty is part of the Scout code and, Joe, you're a good Scout." I picked up the change and went over to Max. I told him I found it on the floor near the register. I couldn't believe it, he said, "You got the job." How cool is that? He told me that being honest was admirable and that I was the type of kid he wanted around his store. He remembered dropping it earlier in the day when he was giving a customer change. I thought to myself he probably wouldn't have remembered it and wondered what would have happened if I didn't say anything and just pocketed it. Was it a test?

Max told me to go home and come back on Wednesday. It really like him. He's a cool guy and now I've got a paying job. I'm going to be rich. I couldn't wait to get home and tell Ma and Dad.

When I got home, dinner was left on the stove. I went into the living room to tell them all about my day at the Columbia Cash Market. Dad and Ma were watching TV. I walked in all excited with the news and Dad's first comment was, "You're in the way of the TV. What do you want?" I told him that I got the job. He said, "That's nice. We'll probably start charging room and board next week. Now go eat your supper so we can watch our show."

I'm sitting up in my room wondering why I even tell them anything. They really don't care what I do as long as I don't disturb their TV shows.

I can't get the change thing out of my head. Today was the second time I 'fessed up and told the truth. Usually I lie to protect myself from a good beating. It felt weird to be honest, but boy did it pay off—I got the job and it was because I told the truth. Hmmm. It's very different outside this house. Not everybody is looking to beat my butt or not interested in what I do. I can't wait to go back to work. I wonder when I get paid.

I think I'll spend my entire paycheck on candy and comic books. Dad couldn't have been serious about charging me room and board. He doesn't charge Randy, but maybe that's because Randy is his buddy. I'm Joe the dog, the one who gets the scraps off the table, who gets kicked around when someone needs to take out their anger or needs to feel good making me feel small.

Maybe someday I'll turn out like Honest Abe Lincoln or George Washington, who was honest enough to admit to cutting down the cherry tree. We don't have a cherry tree, but I don't think I really want to be too honest at home yet.

I think I'll try this Honest Abe thing away from the house. I can see it now. Me walking down the street in New York City. I notice that the well-dressed businessman in front of me drops his wallet as he's trying to put it in his back pocket. He doesn't realize what happened. I run up and pick up the wallet. It's filled with thousand dollar bills. Wow!

I don't even give it a second thought because I live by the Boy Scout code and I'm Honest Joe. I run after the man and finally catch up with him, out of breath. I pull on his coat sleeve and say, "Hey, mister, you dropped your wallet." He turns to me and says, "Well, thanks. It looks like all the money is still in it. You're an honest kid." I smile and agree. He says, "Do you know who I am?" I look, but his face isn't familiar and I shake my head. He says, "I'm Bill Gates." Wow! Mr. Software himself is standing in front of me. How cool can that be? He says, "I want men like you working in Microsoft. Do you have a job?" I tell him I'm working at the Columbia Cash Market. He says, "Well I have a Vice President's job in Honest Customer Relations if you want it. It pays $200,000.00 a year. You get a big fancy office and ten secretaries. It's all yours if you want it."

Just call me Mr. Vice President.

Journal Entry 32 - November 30

I'm so confused I don't know what to do. Usually I just take my beating and move on without telling anyone 'cause I don't think people really care, and even if they did care, I think the bully will just keep on picking on me and it could even get worse.

Now that I'm in seventh grade I go to a much bigger school and there are a lot more kids. Which means more potential bullies. Since I have a part-time job, I have more money than most kids. I try to make friends by buying candy and giving it out. The name Yubbie seems to be the only name I have. I can't seem to escape it no matter where I go. Maybe my parents should change my birth certificate to say Yubbie. One teacher even accidentally called me that. He could tell by the mean stare I gave him that it wasn't a name I like to be called. At least he apologized and called me Joe.

Today I was walking toward the back of the school to have a cigarette. I'm happy I have a job because I can afford to pay for my own smokes and I don't have to steal money from Ma's purse any more. As I went around the corner, a pair of hands grabbed my shirt and threw me up against the dumpster. I immediately had a flash and thought it was Vinnie.

But it wasn't Vinnie. I was eyeball to eyeball with this big stocky kid called Hank. Three of his buddies stood nearby. How come they always have a bunch of buddies with them? Hank's face was red and his breath was gross. He pushed me up against the Dumpster. "Yubbie", he said. "I see ya going around giving other kids candy. You got some for me?" Like I'm gonna protect some stupid candy! I took the bag out of my pocket and lifted it to his face. Then he asked for my smokes. He must have seen me in back of the school smoking.

My heart was pounding a million miles an hour, and I could feel my face turning beet red and getting all sweaty. This guy looked meaner than Vinnie, if that was possible. I put my hand in my pocket and took out a partial pack of smokes. "Good boy, Yubbie, good boy." He said it like I was some kind of dog he was training. At least he took his big hands off me to grab the cigarettes. "You're okay. You're okay as long as you keep me in good supply of these." All I could think was that he needed to eat some of my peppermint candies—he was killing me with his breath.

He shoved me backwards, and as my head hit the Dumpster he said, "You're on my turf and me and my buddies rule. Got it?" They all laughed and walked away. I couldn't believe this was happening all over again. I got rid of Vinnie and now I have a new bully in my life, Hank. At least with Vinnie I could avoid him by not going to Anthony's Pool. Hank goes to my school and I'll have to deal with him every single stinking day.

I wanted to puke as I walked back to my classroom. For the rest of the day I thought about Hank and what I should do about it. I can't tell my parents—they're not going to do anything. Who do I tell? I'm not going down to the principal's office, that's for sure. Mr. K. (I can't even pronounce his name—it's something like Ko-kin-cus) is meaner that Hank. The kids call him Ko Ko Nuts. Even his nickname sounds tough. No way he's gonna help me, and I don't need him calling Ma telling her I'm causing problems at school because then I'll get my butt kicked at home.

I'm so frustrated and angry. On the way to work I even cried as I walked down the railroad tracks. Why doesn't this stuff ever stop? Why doesn't it end? I was walking by the flood control walls built years ago to keep the Hoosatonic River from flooding over. They must be thirty feet from the water below. I actually stopped for a minute and thought of jumping in. I stood on the edge of the wall trying to keep my balance, totally freakin' scared, until finally I stepped back on the grass. What a loser! I can't even kill myself because I'm too chicken. I sat on a rock and kept crying.

I didn't feel like going to work but I had to. Picking up my pace, I made it just in time, hurried in, and put on my apron.

"Are you all right, Joe?" Max asked. Maybe he could see I'd been crying. Thinking quick, I said that I have allergies that bother my eyes or maybe I was coming down with a cold. He looked at me and said, "Humpf," as if part of him didn't believe me. For a second I thought of telling Max. I mean, here I was, lying to him on top of everything else. This guy's been nothing but nice to me in the month I've worked for him, and I lie to his face. We've had some nice talks during our Saturday deliveries. He's an easy guy to talk to. I started thinking maybe I would.

Finally I decided I wanted to ask him if he could talk to me, but there were customers in the store and what could he do anyway? I'm Yubbie and I have to live with being Yubbie. Unless I can end it some other way, I'll always be picked on and harassed.

I was stocking shelves when Max came over to me and asked me to make a special delivery with him. It wasn't Saturday, but if he wanted me to help him, sure. He told me to load the station wagon with some boxes and wait in the car.

We delivered the groceries to Mrs. Katz's house. As we were coming back to the store, Max pulled over and parked on East Street in an area that overlooked the valley. It's one of my favorite views with all the mountain ranges on the horizon.

Max turned to me and said, "Joe, it's none of my business, but

I think there's something wrong with you today. You're awfully quiet and I sense that something's eating at you." He didn't fall for my allergies line. He said, "Sometimes you have to get things off your chest," and then asked if there was anything I wanted to talk about.

It was like he read my mind. When he asked me that, I suddenly realized that no one had ever asked me before. Heck, yeah, I definitely had something to talk about. Like the floodgates of the Hoover Dam opening up, I started crying. I told him I wanted to die.

You'd think a grown-up would freak out about that kind of thing, tell me not to be stupid. But Max didn't tell me not to be stupid. He just said, "Joe, tell me about it." I couldn't look at him, I was crying too hard. He patted me on the shoulder and said it was okay to cry, that I'm in a lot of pain. He didn't know the half of it. I still cried and I still didn't look at him, but I started to tell my story. And I didn't stop until I told him every awful thing that ever happened to me in my whole awful life.

The amazing thing is, he still didn't freak out or anything. He said, "Wow. Joe, that was very painful, I can tell." He said it's clear that I've been living in a really tough and desperate world for many years. What's weird is, he apologized for the bullies. Not like he was saying they were sorry, but that he was sorry that someone as nice as me had to experience those awful things. And he said he thinks it must be miserable to feel so alone. Yeah, it is miserable. Then he made me promise him something. He made me promise not to hurt myself. If I feel this bad again, I'm supposed to talk to him. Even if that means coming in on my days off so we can talk.

It was the first time I ever told anyone my feelings. Even with Mary Lou I didn't say all that much. I didn't want her thinking I was a total loser. Now, after talking to Max, I actually feel relieved. It's not like he did anything, he just sat there and listened, but still, it feels like a ton of bricks is off my shoulders. I'd swear I was carrying that load for years. Max seemed like he cared, and now someone else knows how I feel.

And Max told me something I never thought about before. He said that all this was only temporary. He said that in time things will change if I choose to change them. He said, get this, that I'm "a good kid—smart, handsome, with all kinds of talent." What is he thinking? I'm fat, ugly, and stupid. How can he see something so different?

I think I made a face or something, because he told me that it doesn't matter what I look like. I'm a human being born with abilities to achieve anything I want. "You are perfect unto yourself. There is no one as special to you as you." I know he heard me snort at that. The guy was blowing smoke up my butt, big time. He pointed his finger at me and said, "You have to learn to love who you are, Joe, just like you are, no matter how much you weigh, no matter what kind of grades you get, no matter what. You're perfect and there's no other Joe like you." You're right about that, I thought.

I want to believe Max. I really want to… but it's all kind of confusing. How can you be perfect unto yourself? How can you love yourself? For some reason I can tell he understands those things better than I ever could. Max is smart. He told me that he rarely talks about what happened to him in the war, but he definitely understood how it felt to live in pain and be harassed. He told me it is a hard burden to carry around on our shoulders and that talking about it sometimes helps. Now <u>that</u> I know. Finally.

He told me that he'd like to talk to me more about it in the future. I agreed. Then he asked to talk to my principal about what happened with Hank. Sure, it would be great if someone stood up for me, but talk to Mr. K.? Good luck with that.

I told Max that I was afraid of the principal and that even if the principal did something to Hank, Hank would probably seek revenge and beat me up. Max told me that you can't give in to bullies. They only pick on people they think won't tell or won't do anything about it. I had to do something about it.

Easy for him to say. Part of me wanted so badly to have him make that call. But the rest of me was afraid of a butt whoopin'. So I argued that maybe it had been a one-time thing and that Hank wouldn't bother me any more.

Max didn't agree and he left me with these words: "Joe, you have a right to be left alone. You have a right to get an education without interruption or stress. You have the right to live life without fear of intimidation. These are your birth rights and that is why I joined the military—to defend your right to live in peace without oppression."

I told him I would see what happened, and he made me promise him that if it happened again I would let him know. I agreed.

As we drove back to the store, Max continued to talk to me. I felt a lot better by the time we got back. His last words to me were, "Joe, there are a number of things I would like to talk to you about if you like. I'm not your ma or dad. I'm just someone who cares. Sometimes life brings people together with a purpose in mind. Maybe that's why you were sent to me." Then he thanked me for sharing my story with him.

I'm so tired tonight. I can barely write, but I had to. The things Max said were pretty amazing and I don't want to forget them. I never want to forget them.

Journal Entry 33 - January 15

I took a chance today and I think it'll pay off.

I was called into Mr. K's office. At first I thought, Shoot, what did I do wrong? I'd already had a bad enough couple of days, with Hank shaking me down a second time, only this time for not only my smokes but all my money, too. I thought Max said this kind of life was only temporary. It seemed like it would go on forever.

I'd gone to work yesterday after Hank's attack, all upset. On my way I thought of what Max had said the last time this happened. I wondered if I really should tell him or not. I didn't go down to the floodwalls this time, though, and I didn't cry. I just thought of what was going to happen if I told Max. Would he go and beat Hank up, catching him off guard as he was walking home and beat the snot out of him? Would he call my parents? I don't know what would happen if he did that. Or would Max call my principal and tell him what happened?

A part of me was still scared. If Hank got in trouble, would he come after me and beat me up? If I make trouble for Ma and Dad, would the Torture Chamber Master come out of the dungeon? Would the principal tell Max to mind his business and tell him it's the parents' duty to call? A million thoughts ran through my mind.

When I walked in and saw Max, I knew what I had to do. Not telling him would be like lying. And it would be breaking my promise. So I went up to him and asked if we could speak for a minute before I started stocking. He put down his carving knife, picked up the meat, and placed it back in the cooler below. He took off his apron and led me to his office.

I was really nervous. I was taking a chance on Max. Things could go really, really bad for this, and that's the truth. He told me to close the door and take a seat. I explained what happened at school. When I was done, I asked him what he was going to do? "Are you gonna go beat him up with some of your martial arts?" I said it like I was kidding, kind of. But I really wasn't. I wanted him to bash in Hank's head.

"No, no, no," he said. He told me I did the right thing by telling an adult and that he planned on contacting my principal and explaining what happened. I figured it would be better if he'd just beat up Hank.

Then he asked to contact Ma and Dad. Yikes again.

I explained to him that my folks weren't going to do anything about it and that my dad might beat me just for making a fuss. Dad doesn't like to have anyone bother him when he comes home after a long day. He just likes it quiet. No way I want to get in trouble with him. Max then asked me about my dad and the beatings I get. That sounded like the worst idea ever. Telling someone about that would only get my dad mad. And I said that to Max. I was ready to bolt by then, because I really, really didn't want Dad mad. Max agreed to leave that idea alone, for now at least. He'd still contact my principal. I was okay with that.

One thing I like about Max is how he knows just what to say. He told me, "You were brave today. It took guts to stand up and tell me. I won't let you down."

So by the time I walked into Mr. K's office this morning and told his secretary I was reporting as I was told, I figured out that Max had probably called the school.

After a minute, Mr. K's office door opened and who do I see but Hank coming out office with a man and woman. I guess they were his parents. Hank gave me a dead cold stare. Swell, just like I'd thought, Hank was planning to kill me the next time he saw me. I felt lost and helpless and so sorry I'd told Max anything.

Mr. K's secretary told me to go in. There was Ma sitting in a chair next to the principal's desk. What was she doing there? It was getting worse! I panicked inside, thinking, "Oh, I'm going to get a whipping tonight." Worse yet, I had told Max that my dad beats me. I hope he didn't tell the principal. My dad might kill me before Hank has a chance. Stupid, stupid me for opening my big, fat mouth. That's what I thought at that second, anyway. All those fears went out the window when Ma smiled at me. I nearly tripped, then and there.

Mr. K. told me to take a seat. He said he'd received a call that morning that had him very concerned. Turns out he's known Max for years and knew he would only call about something serious. He asked me if what Max said was true, did Hank have a confrontation with me in the schoolyard twice? I nodded yes.

He didn't look happy about that. I waited for him to tell Ma to take me home and never bring me back. But he didn't do that. He explained to me that he had to contact Ma because it was the law. He said that I'm not the first student Hank has picked on. Hank's been a troublemaker for the last two years. And then Mr. K. went and started sounding like Max: "At least you had enough courage to tell someone. Most kids don't because they are afraid. You did the right thing."

I couldn't believe what I was hearing. I did the right thing. Amazing. And what do I get for doing the right thing? No Hank, that's what I get! Hank got his last warning at the end of the last school year and so with my complaint now, that's it—he's out for good. Plus, he's getting this "incident" filed with the local police department and if he's dumb enough to come after me then he'll have to go to jail. I almost cried again, right in the principal's office. He was telling me it was over. I didn't have to be afraid of Hank anymore. The law would protect me.

Then Mr. K. sent me home, but not because I was busted. It was like a break, to help me relax. He said that if any student in his school touches me, then I'm supposed to go to him immediately and he'll take care of it. He looked like the mean Ko Ko Nuts we all knew when he said that. "Bullying will not be tolerated in my school," he said. And I totally believed him. I nodded again as this giant of a man got up from his chair and came over to Ma and me.

He thanked Ma for coming in and told her that he'd do

everything in his power to make sure that I'd be safe in school. Ma was like me, nodding but not saying a lot of anything. I was a little worried about what she'd say in the car. She'd smiled when I walked in, but I didn't really know what that meant.

On the way home Ma asked why I never told them about what happened. She told me that she'd never let anyone hurt me. I thought, "You let Dad beat the crap out of me and I'm gonna think you'll protect me? Am I on a different planet?" I didn't say it, though. She really did seem like she cared.

After supper I went up to my room. I could hear Ma and Dad arguing downstairs. I figured she was telling him that she had to come to my school today. I waited to see if I was going to get a visit from my dad or the Torture Chamber Master. Neither one came to my room.

I think I'm happy over this whole thing. I know I brought a lot of attention to myself and I hope it pays off. I hope I never see Hank again. And it's all because of Max. Mad Max. Huh, I don't get that nickname at all. There's nothing crazy about Max.

In my mind, Max is America's best. I can see him now—Max the decorated soldier deciding to come out of his retirement to take on one more important mission at the request of the President himself.

They have to fly him a hundred miles behind enemy lines. It's a suicide mission if he fails. He's entering the middle of the enemy's green zone, where all the tactical decisions are made. The airplane has to fly under radar in order to escape detection.

Max waits for the green light to appear on the plane monitor. He doesn't even think about the risk—all he knows is that he has a mission and he'll succeed. The light turns green and he makes his jump into the jungle. He takes off all his gear and loads all his weapons. He knows he doesn't want to use them 'cause he wants to avoid detection.

He makes his way into the compound like a church mouse

making its way through cracks and crevices. So far, so good. He sees the detention center where his mission's target is located. As he crosses the compound, one of the enemy soldiers spots him. He takes out his trusty ninja knife and throws it, nailing the soldier's throat. The soldier falls to the ground in silence.

Max gets inside and follows the tracker beam on his GPS locator. He goes down corridor after corridor, slicing the throat of every guard on the way. He makes it undetected. He puts a silent hydrogen rope bomb on the door lock and it melts through. He opens the door and sees his target—me. I'm wounded and he has to carry me out on his shoulder. He's a strong ranger with arms like the Terminator, and he lifts me real easily.

He runs down the corridors to get us out, using his 9-millimeter machine gun with a silencer on it. The guards are falling like flies. Once out in the compound he sees a truck parked next to the building. He knows he has to make time to rendezvous with the helicopter pick-up. He places me in the front seat and jumps in. As he starts the truck, the guards on the walls notice him. They start shooting their machine guns as he puts the pedal to the metal and speeds out of the compound, breaking through the gate to freedom.

We make it to the pick-up location with a trail of enemy soldiers, tanks, and jeeps hot on our trail. The copter lands. Max carries me and places me inside. He stands on the landing gear holding a machine gun with one hand, shooting at the enemy as we take off to safety. I'm rescued by my hero—Mad Max.

Journal Entry 34 - January 18

Max is a really smart guy. He talks about so many deep things. He makes a lot of sense. I wish someone had told me all this stuff before.

Today is the Saturday after Hank got kicked out of school. I hadn't seen Max since he went to Principal K. So the first thing I did when I went to work was thank Max for helping me out. I filled him in on the details. He was glad I won't have to worry about Hank anymore.

We made a lot of deliveries today, and in between each delivery we talked. He asked me a question and I thought, Duh! The question was, "Why do you think kids pick on you?" Because I'm fat, ugly, and stupid, that's why. I couldn't believe I had to say that out loud. But Max makes saying anything okay, so I answered him.

He didn't believe me. He said I'm not stupid. He's right that I've done a real good job working for him. But when he said that I've shown him I'm pretty smart...well, I don't know about that. I like the sound of it, though. No one ever said that other than Danny's dad.

The thing is, how can you be smart when your school grades stink and everyone in your family thinks you're stupid? Max didn't have an answer for that. He just asked me another question: Did I do my homework? I had a feeling he wouldn't like my answer. He seems like the kind of guy who likes homework. But he doesn't understand how our house works. Ma and Dad don't care how I do at school. Heck, Dad didn't finish high school and Ma couldn't speak English until she was seven years old since that's when she arrived from Poland, and she barely finished high school herself. So sometimes I do it and other times... oh, well!

Then Max twisted that in a way I never thought of before. He thinks that I'm responsible for my bad grades not because I'm stupid but because I don't do the required work. And he thinks I don't do the work because my folks don't encourage me. Maybe he's right. Maybe people think I'm stupid just because I don't try hard enough and nobody at my house seems to care. It makes a kind of sense, now that I think about it.

Then he went to the 'ugly' and I didn't want to talk about that! I mean, you can't blame being ugly on anybody but yourself. You just are or you aren't. But Max being Max, he had to ask about it. "What makes you think you're ugly?" Uh, the MIRROR!

But Max didn't deserve an answer like that. He's a good guy. So I tried to be good about saying it, thoughtful, like he is. I tried real hard to word it just right. "When I look in the mirror I see an ugly boy staring back at me. He's worthless and hopeless. My brothers and the other kids also tell me how ugly I am. They see me every day, so they know." For the first time in our deliveries, I thought about wanting out of the car. I didn't like talking about this. It hurts enough to think about it.

Big surprise: Max doesn't think I'm ugly at all. He said I'm a handsome young man who has so much more growing to do. At first I thought, "He has to say that." But then he started staying stuff that has me thinking. I mean, he makes a lot of sense, Max does. He said I'm ugly maybe because I think I'm ugly. Huh? I don't see what <u>thinking</u>'s got do with it. You either are ugly or you aren't, right? All this stuff he says about how the way we look at ourselves determines how other people look at us and react to us—well, it's pretty confusing. I'm not telling people to think I'm ugly. They just look at me and see it.

But Max says it's not that way. He says the reason bullies pick on me isn't because of the way I look. Sure, since I look a little different they might target me. But mostly the bullying is all about having power over someone. He said the bully tries to get this power over someone who doesn't fit in with how most people look—and that I'm allowing them the power.

This sat me back a bit. I said, "What?"

"Yes," he said. "It's the truth, and you proved it."

I swear, I was totally convinced that this guy must be off the deep end. Maybe something happened to him when he was at war. But how does that explain what he said next? It does make sense, when he says it like he does. He said the bullies reach out for a reaction. If you stand up to them—like maybe laughing off what they say—then they don't have any power over you. Or if that doesn't work and you tell an adult like I did, they lose all their power. I guess that's true. I mean, if I look at it that way, then Hank lost his power over me when the principal kicked him out of school and told the police, didn't he? So all these mean bullies can only have power over me if I let them. That sounds nice and all, but it's not that easy. When's the last time Max had to stand up to anyone? Max says I just have to have confidence in myself that I'm not going to give in to bullies. I have to stand and say no. The bully will usually turn around and try to find someone else to pick on.

Why hasn't anyone ever told me that? How could I argue? So far Max has been right about everything. I don't have any confidence. I don't feel like I'm worth anything. I'm scared to stand up and say no because I don't want to get a beating just like Dad would give me.

I've heard people say that bullies are the ones with the problem, not me. But it never made any sense to me. Then here was Max telling me that bullying means something's happening in the bully's life that makes him want to have power over others. Like maybe he has a difficult home life. Well, when Max said that, I figured he really didn't understand after all. He doesn't have any idea about how difficult a home life can be. If that's really how it is, then *I* should be a bully.

I was thinking like this when Max said something that really got my attention. He said that lots of times bullies have parents who beat them or do drugs or drink, or that the bullies see others in their life get beat on, and that the bullies can't do anything about it but be angry so they turn around and look for ways to get rid of their anger. Maybe that's why Trevor's so mean?

The more I think about it, the more I think Max's right that this isn't all me. I need to keep that in my head. He says I have great potential and that I just have to allow myself the chance to achieve it. I do like the idea of standing strong and not letting others get away with picking on me. I did the right thing with Hank and it worked out. Maybe if I act confident, then bullies really will leave me alone. I asked Max if he really thought that would work. That's when he finally told me why they called him Mad Max.

When he was with the 101st Airborne, Max was kind of a small guy compared to the rest. All the guys used to pick on him because of his size. He laughed it off and never let it really bother him. Once they were behind enemy lines. The fighting was fierce and their replacements were delayed. They started to run out of ammo and had to fight hand to hand. It was terrible. He didn't remember exactly what happened, but those who survived told him that he went berserk and fought ruthlessly, taking out many of the enemy. From that day on his nickname was Mad Max.

He told me this story because he wanted me to know that he understands being picked on. And he found out himself that the way you present yourself makes the difference. No matter where he went afterward, his name would make people get out of his way. So he started always walking strong and with confidence and nobody ever picked on him again.

It's so different having someone like Max talk to me. He makes a lot of sense. Maybe I'll start bringing my schoolwork home and try to get better grades, like he says. He even offered that if I can't figure something out on my homework and I can't find anyone to help me, that I can come ask him. He says I have to study and get a good education if I want to make my life different than my dad's. I do! I don't want to be stuck in a factory making roller chains when it's 110 degrees in the summer. I'd rather be sitting in an air-conditioned office on the top of a tall building overlooking the city. I want an office as big as the school cafeteria, and a desk bigger than our couch. I'm gonna have my own bar, living room, and all kinds of fancy doodads just like in the Oval Office at the White House. I'll have ten secretaries and just sit behind my desk smoking Cuban cigars and drinking stuff from crystal bottles—all because I did my homework. Cool!

Journal Entry 35 - May 1

I've been doing a lot of laughing lately—as in "laughing it off." I think it's paying off. Not so many kids pick on me the same way any more. It still hurts when they do, but they don't know it. Most times, just like Max said, they back off and stop. Max knows a lot about things, that's for sure.

Yesterday was the school picnic. I made some new friends during the school year—Rick and Mike. They're a lot of fun. Rick and Mike both like to play baseball, ride their bikes, and hang around the Hoosac Street School and play cards. They never call me Yubbie—just Joe.

My grades have been better. Report cards came out a couple of weeks ago and I got my first B and four Cs. That's amazing for me. Usually I get all Ds and maybe even an F. Maybe the better grades are because I'm keeping up with my promise to Max. Just like I said I would, I've started to take home the work I don't complete at school. I'm finishing it after supper. I don't spend a lot of time on it or anything, but I think that a little more makes a difference—or I'm just getting smarter. My grades prove it. For the first time in forever, I showed Ma my report card. She was happy with my marks. I tried to tell Dad at supper. Here I was, all excited about the results and his comment was, "Good, keep it up." It kind of popped my bubble. I mean, who doesn't want their dad to get all jazzed over a good report card? But at least he said it was good.

Max, though, he got jazzed about it. He said, "Wow! Great job. That's fantastic, Joe. I'm proud of you. I knew you could do it." He even gave me five bucks as a bonus for a great report card. I am so happy I work for Max. My dad could take a few lessons from him.

Rick and Mike invited me to walk up to this huge picnic the school was hosting at the Mawufka grounds. There would be tons of food and games and a band and everyone from school was going to be there. They were walking up with Kathy, Joanne, Cindy, and Irene. How could I say no? Kathy is my dream girl. She's so pretty. I say hi to her every day. I never get time to talk to her, though. Well, that's not totally true. The thing is, I'm afraid to. She's beautiful and all the boys in my class try to date her. What chance would a fat guy like me have asking her to the movies? Heck, there are some things that you know ain't gonna happen. It's like expecting Angelina Jolie to say yes to a date with me. No way, no how.

So when they asked me to join them, I jumped at the chance. It was a great day. We had so much fun on the way up. It takes about a half hour to walk to the picnic grounds, or we had the choice of taking a bus. Who wants to take a bus when you have a chance to be with Kathy?

We had such a good time. I tried to tell all kinds of stories to make the girls laugh. They all seemed to like me. It was great. I was hoping by the time we got to the picnic grounds that maybe I could get Kathy to like me enough to actually have a soda with me and talk. Now that I work, I have all kinds of money and I could show her a good time.

In between my stories I tried to think of how I would ask her or at what point during the walk I could talk to her alone. My little brain was hard at work trying to figure out how I was going to do it. Rick and Mike weren't trying to date her, so I didn't have to worry about them. They were neighbors and friends with Kathy, so that left me an open field. I just had to wait for the perfect moment.

We got to the picnic grounds and checked in at the registration table. We needed tickets to pay for any food or activity so that no one had to deal with money once we got in. I bought a whole bunch of tickets so that I could buy as much soda, candy, and hot dogs for both Kathy and me as we wanted. As I was walking away from the table I thought, "How am I going to ask her?" Maybe I could tell a joke and as she laughed say, "Would you like to join me in a soda?" Corny. Maybe I should just flat out walk up to her and say, "Hey, babe, you want to join me for the ride of your life?" Aw, man, have I been watching too many movies, or what? It's not like I had any other great ideas, though. Man, I wanted to talk to her. She has that little sparkle in her eyes, just like Mary Lou did. Was there a chance?

After having a soda to build up my courage, I decided on the direct approach. I was going to buy two sodas and go right up to her and say, "Kathy, I bought this soda for you. Would you like to take a walk?" I could see her standing with a bunch of girls over by the band. How do I get her away from all those girls? I walked over very slowly, trying to build up the confidence I needed to ask her.

By the time I made it to her I was practically crying I was so afraid. I hate that feeling. I felt like puking up the soda I just drank. I kinda made my way beside her, took a deep breath, and said, "Kathy, here's a soda. They gave me two by mistake. You want one?" She politely said yes. I hated myself so much. I just couldn't get the right words out. I was scared and all of Max's words about acting confident came back to me and I felt like I was being bashed over the head. What a loser! Now what was I going to do?

I was going to make Max proud, that's what. I stood there watching the band set up and took another deep breath and said,

"Kathy, would you like to take a walk?" It came out! I couldn't believe it! Part of me was happy but part of me wanted to take it back, just knowing what was going to happen next. And I was right: rejection! Kathy turned to me giggling and said, "I really can't. My boyfriend Kenny is in the band."

Darn! The humiliation! If I could be an ice sculpture, I would have let the sun melt me so I could then disappear into the ground. And what's with the giggle? Was she was giggling to be nice or giggling at how impossible it would be for a fat guy like me to get her to take a walk?

I slowly moved backwards and walked away feeling really sad and lonely. I was so lame to think that Kathy would even give me the time of day, never mind want to spend time with me. I went over to the grill and bought two hot dogs, two hamburgers, two orders of fries, and two sodas. I put tons of ketchup and mustard on everything and carried my loaded my tray out to the baseball field. All by myself, I watched the kids play and devoured my food. I sat back, stuffed like a pig and feeling nauseous.

After a while I decided to take a walk in the woods. It was so peaceful. I walked wondering and wondering what I'm trying so hard for? All this homework and asking girls out and being rejected. I'm just going to be old and alone and working in a rolling chain factory. I walked for hours and eventually ended up at my house.

It's almost bed time. I guess at least I didn't let Max down. I tried with Kathy. I got up the guts, and I tried. But I was rejected again. There's no hope for me. I'll never find a girl who wants to marry me and have kids with me. What I really need is a change of body and a change of brain. Kenny is blonde with blue eyes and slim. Whatever made me think that Kathy would choose Yubbie?

Journal Entry 36 - June 18

School is out and I'm lovin' it. I had a great week. This job has really been worth it. Not only did I meet someone who helps me figure things out, but I got BUCKS!

The last report card came out for the year. My eyes almost dropped out of my head. I got three Bs this time and two Cs. My best report card ever! So I guess it's official: I'm not stupid. I can really get good grades if I try. I did all my homework after my last report card, trying to figure out if I did more would I get better grades, and it worked. I can't believe it!

I told Ma when I got home from school, but I couldn't wait to go to work and show Max. I knew he'd be so proud of me. I walked in and ran toward the back of the store to his office and shouted like some little kid, "Max, check this out!" It really did feel like Christmas or something. Max jumped up from his chair and said, "Incredible, Joe! I knew I had you pegged right. You're a really smart kid. I'm impressed." He's proud of me. Max is proud of me. I told him that I did all my homework just like he said and didn't miss one and that's why my grades are good. He said, "Doesn't that feel great when you accomplish something?" Heck, yeah! "All right," he said, "this calls for a celebration." Woohoo!

We busted out the ice cream and cake, right there in the store. Max got his brothers from the meat-cutting corner and we all stuffed our faces. It was so cool. Here they had all this meat to cut but they were taking a break to toast me with scoops of Cookie Dough. I wanted to cry. Tears filled my eyes just like the night I got my ten patches at camp.

I'll never forget today. These guys in the store made me feel like I am somebody. They don't even know how much. I swear, I've landed on the moon. This was a different world for me. Nobody at my house ever did anything like this for me.

Max could see that I was all goopy-eyed. I didn't want him thinking I was a baby, not after all this, so I swiped my sleeve over my eyes. Max pulled my hand away from my face. He said, "Joe, you're doing a great job and you should be proud of yourself. There's nothing wrong with shedding a tear. It's okay for men to cry." Now I know I'm on another planet. My dad would've swatted the back of my head for crying, not stopped me from wiping the tears away. I sniffled a couple of times and told him thank you. But I didn't mean just for the cake, I meant for everything. I wish Max was my dad. And that's what I told him. He patted me on the shoulder and said, "That would sure be an honor." Working with Max is the best.

I've saved up enough money from my job to buy what I've wanted for such a long time—an electric guitar and amplifier. I know exactly the one I'm going buy. It's red and really cool looking.

After I was done stocking shelves, Max came over and told me we had to make a delivery. On the way, I told Max what happened with Kathy rejecting me and all. He said I shouldn't get all twisted about it. It's not rejection, she just said no. She didn't call me any names and I don't know why she was giggling. Which is a good point.

Max had a lot of good points. Like that a girl saying no isn't a personal insult. There isn't anything wrong with me. If a girl judges a guy only on his appearance, then she's being superficial. I know that means just looking at the surface. It's messed up when people judge by outside things. It's what's inside a person that really counts. That's what matters when it comes to getting along.

Max says I have more to offer than guys who just have good looks. I guess. I mean, yeah, I'm nice and I can be funny. And I do like to help people because I care. I went to see Vinnie in the hospital, didn't I? And if I had a girlfriend, I would be totally loyal. And honest. I don't even swipe my ma's money anymore, and I only lie to her and Dad to save myself from a butt whooping. Maybe it is as easy as Max says. Maybe I just have to keep on trying until the right girl says yes.

Here's what I don't get: How come Max can see so many good things about me that nobody else sees? He only sees me at work. Does he possess special powers? Can he look inside someone and figure them out? However he does it, he's always right. And if he says I can be confident and just keep asking and then something good will happen, then I guess it will. I trust Max.

Maybe it's like when I thought about Vinnie getting crushed on the football field and then he was. If you think about something long and hard enough, it happens. Wouldn't that be neat! I think I'll go to bed thinking about being a rock star. Me up on a stage with my brand new red electric guitar and the audience going crazy. My band and I would crank out some serious tunes and everyone would applaud. And at the end of the concert, they'd break out the cake, ice cream, and soda and call for a celebration. Wild!

Journal Entry 37 - July 6

BANG! I got the key to the city today. Max told me about the power of my mind—and it works. Wow! It's really cool.

It really started three weeks ago when I went to work on a Saturday. Rick and Mike invited me to go on a fifty-mile bike ride. I know, it sounds crazy, but I'd kind of been bragging about doing fifty miles on my ten speed and it being a piece of cake. I gotta learn to keep my big mouth shut! It gets me into all sorts of trouble. But it's so cool having people get impressed when I tell them stuff like that. Who am I hurting?

Me, I guess. That's who I'm hurting. Specifically, I'm hurting my butt. The most I've ever ridden at any one time is six miles, and that's long enough to be on a bike seat. Usually I leave from the house and ride my bike to Dairy Queen six miles away in another town. Then of course I eat my double-dipped triple-decker chocolate ice cream and peddle myself home another six miles. That makes twelve. Still, twelve is hardly fifty miles. Fifty miles on a bike seat? The pain!

Mike and Rick were planning to do the bike ride in three weeks. I told them yes. I mean, what choice did I have? I thought maybe I could train for it in those three weeks, in secret. But how do you train for something that big? I knew Max had done marathons and stuff. So of course I went to him.

Max figured out a training program for me. We knew I could do twelve miles in a day thanks to riding to and from the Dairy Queen, so he had me start with that. Twelve miles a day, every day. After three days, I was supposed to take a day off to rest and build energy and then go out for a twenty-two mile trip. I just about passed out when he said that. "Just make sure you keep drinking a lot of water," he said. Yeah, like that would make the extra ten miles go by like nothing. Yikes!

Here's the routine Max gave me: three days at twelve miles,

then a day off, then twenty-two miles, then a day off, then back to three days at twelve miles, then another day off, then THIRTY miles, blah, blah, blah. He said if I did that, then it would be no problem to do fifty miles.

Then he got all goofy and acted like he had some big old secret. He leaned in and whispered to me, "Here's the key to the city—the most important tool of tools, and it's all in your head." Seriously, Max was losing it. I couldn't figure it out any other way. The key to the city? But then, Max is always right. Right? Give me the key, Max: "The greatest tool you have," he said, all serious, "is the power of your thought." Okay, I thought, put this man in a jacket and take him to the funny farm. Sure it kind of seemed like I'd sent Vinnie to the hospital just by thinking it, but I know down deep that life doesn't work that way. Now, here was Max telling me it did? Nut case, for sure.

I really like Max and I didn't want to be dissing him or anything, so I listened when he explained what he meant. See, our thoughts have a powerful energy. When we see something in our mind, see it like it's here right now, we feel a certain way about it. That feeling puts out an energy that helps the thing come into our lives some day. Kind of like a magnet. What we think about attracts those things into our lives. That's why Max always says he feels great—because then he will feel great.

Sounds like hocus pocus to me. You have to believe that whatever it is you want is yours to have. And you have to act like you already do have it. Totally weird.

I tried to see how that would help me ride fifty miles, but I just couldn't. So Max gave me an assignment. He said I had to go to bed every night and picture myself riding my bicycle on the fifty-mile route. I had to see myself going up the hills like they were nothing and blasting my way down the hills. I could even picture myself blowing right past Rick and Mike. If I did what Max was telling me to do, I'd be putting out the thought energy to make that happen. And I had to feel it while I imagined it, totally act like I just passed the fifty-mile mark and get all freaked out and happy.

Max had no idea who he was talking to. I can picture myself doing <u>anything</u>! Why stop at fifty miles? Why not picture a hundred? Now <u>that</u> I could do. So I did.

Every day I did my training miles. Every night I dreamed about the fifty mile ride. Max warned me not to let any doubt creep in. It works against you when you do that. You gotta believe it, for real, totally. Doubt totally torpedoes the positive thoughts. Doubting was a big no-no.

And guess what? Max was right. All that brain whammy stuff worked!

Rick and Mike are in good shape. They both play sports at school and Mike even got a letter last year for his football jacket. Even with all my imagining I never thought I'd be able to keep up with them. They didn't think so, either. Mike told me that they would stop and break whenever I felt I needed to. I just had to let them know.

We started out today early in the morning. We went twelve miles on little rolling hills. I stayed in back so I didn't have to worry about slowing them down. It was pretty easy. Then we came to the mountain roads. These roads went up into the hills that were pretty steep.

The first one was three miles long. We stopped before the climb just to take a water break and get ready. I never asked them to stop. I told them I felt great and was ready to go. It wasn't just the brain whammy stuff—I really meant it. I felt really good. Twelve miles is nothing! We started the climb—and I was keeping up with them! I was a little out of breath and that's because I probably smoke too much, but I was able to hold my own. I stood up on the bike and rode to the top.

On the way down, just like I had seen in my mind, I went

blasting down the hill, passing both of them. Maybe because I'm heavier? Whyever. I'll take it.

We hit the bottom and then had to go up the next mountain. We did this over and over. Each time, they would catch up with me as we climbed. My legs burned on hills. I just kept picturing myself cruising up and thinking, "Burn, baby, burn!" I wasn't stopping unless I got hit by a bus. Then on the down side I would zoom like a rocket, blowing right by them.

We hit the twenty-five mile mark and Rick signaled a stop. We pulled into a convenience store. My legs were burning a little, but otherwise it wasn't that bad. I drank two bottles of water and ate a couple of bagels. Carbs. That's what Max told me to eat when we had a break.

Back on the road. My legs were burning more. I chanted, "I can do it, I can do it," in my head. The burning kind of disappeared in the background. It was amazing. I was keeping up without all that much trouble. My butt didn't even hurt that much from the bike seat. We were forty miles out when we pulled over again. They asked me if I was okay, and I told them I felt fine. I think they were surprised I was able to keep up. What, did they think I wouldn't be able to? The nerve! I am Joe, hear me roar! I felt invincible.

The last ten miles were the toughest. My legs were really burning, but I just kept concentrating on the fifty-mile mark. I broke out more of Max's mind tricks by telling myself, "We're there! I did it, I did it!" We weren't there, but he said to believe it was happening now and then it would happen. Sure enough, we came rolling right back into town. We'd gone in a full circle. A FIFTY MILE circle! I was so happy! Totally, freaking-out excited. It actually felt the way I had imagined it in my mind. Max was right—our thoughts have the power to bring stuff to us. I'll totally have to use this for other things.

The excitement is kind of wearing off now. Full on exhaustion is creeping in, actually. Still, I had to do one thing before going to sleep—call Max and tell him I did it. So that's what I did just a few minutes ago. He answered the phone at the store. I knew he'd be there. The store closes real late. "It's me," I told him. "The fifty mile biker." He cheered right into the phone. He said he never had any doubt in his mind. And then he said the best thing: "You're getting to be quite a successful person, you know."

This thought stuff is really interesting. Instead of trying to go to sleep thinking about crazy things, maybe I'll start thinking about being in a band playing my red electric guitar. I've been practicing almost every day. Maybe if I see myself playing in a band every night and then practice a lot during the day, then someday it will be true. Max says that you have to believe and take action on your belief. It sure beats thinking about escaping or running away. Maybe I'll think about myself being skinny. Won't that be cool? I am! I got the key.

Journal Entry 38 - July 30

I got snagged smoking today by Max. I was kinda shocked at his reaction. Doesn't this guy ever get upset? I've broken things in the store, I've accidentally ruined the meat slicer's blade by using the wrong tool to sharpen it, and I've spilled his coffee all over some important papers. Not a yell, scream, or red in the face angry reaction. Sometimes I think he got hit in the head during his fierce fighting and he short-circuited his brain. My dad would have whooped the tar out of me and left me for dead on a deserted back road if I did all those things in my house. I wonder why Max doesn't? All that brain whammy stuff must be doing something to this guy.

Today I was loading the station wagon to make our deliveries. I told Max I was all set to go and he told me to wait outside. I waited and waited. He didn't come out so I decided to have a smoke. I was halfway through when Max came walking out the door. I panicked and threw the butt on the ground and stepped on it. Instead of freaking out, he looked at me and said, "You could have finished it, Joe."

Oh, no I couldn't. Not in front of him. "I was done anyways." I mostly was.

I was totally embarrassed. Here's a guy who is a super athlete, who eats all these weird health foods, runs every day, and meditates. What was he going to think of me now? I probably break every rule in his book, like eating ice cream, drinking soda instead of bottled water, eating the fat on the Thanksgiving turkey, drinking regular milk instead of nonfat, all that. And now he knows I smoke.

It was a few miles before he brought it up again. "When did you get into that habit?" He said it like he was curious, not like he was getting ready to unload both barrels at me. I had to answer him, of course. Max is the only person I don't lie to. He tells me it's always important to tell the truth, no matter what. To just be me. All my life I've lied to avoid getting beaten by Dad, bullies, my brothers, or to have people think I'm somebody important. With Max it's different. I can be me, and he accepts everything I do without getting mad. So I told him about Bobby at Eagle Camp.

He went from when did I start to why? That was easy enough to answer. I wanted to be accepted by my friend and fit in, that's why. But when he asked if I like it, well, I had to think about that one. Smoking's okay. It makes me feel good. I don't get dizzy from it anymore. I probably run out of breath faster, but so what? I'm not running marathons like him. I didn't tell him that last part. That part, I just thought.

He thanked me for being truthful. "Two things I would like to say about that," he said. I almost groaned out loud. Here it was, the lecture.

Only it didn't turn out to be a lecture. He asked me to do something."Think about the reason you started," he said. I wanted to be accepted and fit in—what's so bad about that? Well, it turns out that wanting to fit in is the same as being afraid of being rejected. Like with Kathy. Max reminded me that I had to realize that I'm okay the way I am. It doesn't matter if people accept me or not. They have a choice to let me become part of their lives or not. I shouldn't have to adjust myself to accommodate them. Real friends will accept me as I am with all my weaknesses and strengths. If they don't, then they aren't good friends.

Then I blurted out the first thing that popped into my head: "Max, you don't understand how it feels to be me." I couldn't believe I just said that. I'd never spoken that way to him. But it's the truth. "All my life, all I ever wanted is to have people and kids like me. That's all I want, just to be somebody." Then I went and got all teary eyed.

"You *are* somebody just the way you are," he said. "You're perfect."

There he went with the "perfect unto yourself" stuff. I have such a hard time understanding that. He says my body is nothing more than a shell and there's much more to me than just my physical being. Well, my shell just happens to be extra large and double wide. I may have special insides and offer many things to the world around me like Max says, but there's no way you could call me perfect. Why does he say those things?

He asked me if Tom and Danny smoke. I sensed a trap. "No," I said. "Do they accept you the way you are?" he asked. And the trap slammed shut! "Yeah," I admitted. "They always have." And that's the honest truth. They are good friends. Max said I should value them, because they have no motive to spend time with me beyond friendship. All the other people, the ones who I have to try to fit in with, they aren't the kinds of friends I should want. They don't appreciate the beauty in my soul, he said. Be kind, be myself, and it will happen. I swear, Max gets me every time. I started blubbering again. I'm such a crybaby sometimes.

It's never been easy for me to make friends. I've always wanted them. Real bad. But does that mean I have to take anyone, no matter how I have to act to fit in with them? I never looked at it that way until Max challenged me on it. Maybe it's like Max's positive thinking stuff. Maybe if I just be friendly but be myself, then those kids that were meant to be my friends will appear. I sure like the sound of it.

Of course, Max didn't forget the cigarette. "Joe, let's talk about smoking." That's pretty much the last thing I wanted to talk about. There's no way he'd be okay with that. And really, after what he said about my reason for starting to smoke, I'm beginning to wonder about it myself. It's true what he says, that it's my body and my life and I have the right to make my own decisions. But then he told me what the decision I was making really was. See, the reason I got dizzy was because when the human body gets smoke in its lungs, chemicals come with it. Tar and nicotine being the worst ones. Tar? That can't be good—they used tar on the roof of my school last year! The dizziness is my body and my brain being deprived of oxygen.

I asked Max how he knows this and his answer shocked me. He was a smoker twenty-five years ago, that's how he knows. I still can't believe it! Max with a cigarette? No way! But the thing is, because of that, he knows what I mean when I say that smoking makes me feel good. He said that's why a lot of people keep smoking, once they start. But it's kind of a trick because that good feeling comes from drugs in the smoke—it's a chemical high. Nicotine is a real, official drug, and our lungs can't deal with it, so it ends up in our blood stream. And here all I thought smoking did make me cough a little.

Max made me get out my smokes and look at the pack. He pointed to the warning label on it. "They don't put that there for decoration," he said. The drugs and chemicals really do give you medical problems like cancer, emphysema, heart disease, and respiratory illnesses—all that stuff they put on the label and more. He told me these things may not kill me, but I won't be able to have an active and happy life. Like bike riding and swimming. None of that.

That's why he stopped. He had health problems after the war and spent a lot of time in the hospital. The doctors told him that he might not ever heal, and he didn't like that. He read every book he could find about healing and learned that the body will heal itself as long as we give it a chance. So he stopped smoking, drinking, and eating junk food. He started exercising, meditating, and eating good, healthy food. It took a long time, but his body did heal. And now he's in the best shape ever.

How could I argue? He made a lot of sense. Max has gone through a lot in his life. Boy, he must be a genius from reading all those books. He should have become a doctor.

Well, it's time to go to bed. I think I am going to give up smoking some day. I want to be like Max—strong, healthy, and tough. I still keep visualizing every night before I fall to sleep that I'm in a band with my red electric guitar. I can see the audience clapping and cheering as my band performs. It feels great to be up on the stage. Better even than smoking.

Journal Entry 39 - August 1

I'm almost there. I'm writing in my journal tonight in my tent. I have to sleep all alone and be by myself in the middle of the woods. It's hard to write with only a Boy Scout flashlight.

It started a couple of weeks ago when I was telling Max about the Boy Scouts. Tom and Danny were going to try for the Order of the Arrow designation. There was an "Ordeal," the beginning step, coming up at Camp Eagle. They told me I should also try it. All three of us recently got our First Class and were eligible.

It sounded a little scary. You have to go out in the woods and kinda be by yourself. You can't talk to anyone during the three-day test. I love to talk. I didn't think I could keep my mouth shut for three whole days. They also give you only a little bit of food. The rest you have to get by eating berries and other things in the woods. I thought about some of those TV reality shows where they have to eat bugs and slugs. I couldn't imagine myself putting those slimy moving things in my mouth. What happens to them when they go into your stomach? The slugs probably set up camp and have baby slugs and before you know it you have families of slugs living in your stomach. No thanks!

I was told that you also had to do projects around the campsite. That was no big deal. I can lash and make anything I want. The whole thing sounded cool, but part of me couldn't imagine being by myself—or worse yet, sleeping alone in a tent. What if something happens like in those movies when out of the dark woods some kind of monster comes and drags you out of your tent by your feet and devours you arm by arm, leg by leg, as you scream and kick. I had my doubts.

I told Max about the Ordeal.

He told me I should try for it. I told him how I felt and he told me that he felt safer in the woods, at night in total darkness, than walking the streets of New York City. People are more dangerous than the animals in the Berkshires. That's a good point! I don't think any bears would be out there waiting to mug me.

I told Max that my Dad had no interest in going to Camp Eagle. Dad reminded me when I asked him that he told me when I joined the Scouts he wasn't going to cart me around or get involved. He has things to do on the weekend. I hate asking my Dad for anything. I try to avoid him. Now that I'm working, I don't even have to sit and eat supper with him every night like a church mouse picking up the crumbs, hoping the big bad cat doesn't hear me munching. He's as mean as ever. When I come home from work he'll be arguing with Ma over something or other. She's usually pretty looped by that time of the day and the antics just keep rolling out. I can't wait for the day I can leave and be on my own.

He asked me if it would make it easier if he went with the other fathers during this three-day event. I couldn't believe it. Why is this guy in my life? What did I do right? I am so thankful that someone above has shown me mercy and sent Max to help me.

It was a deal. If he would come along, then I'd do it. And here I am.

The first night was the worst. There were people around during the day because we really weren't all that spread out. I could see the other scouts throughout the woods building their campsites, and now and then an adult would come through my site to check on my projects. But I couldn't talk to anyone. Not even Max when he came by. So hard! But Max was cool about it, making sure when he walked through that I could see him wink. It was nice knowing he was there backing me up.

It was after supper when the sun went down that things got eerie. There were all kinds of noises coming out of the woods. I could hear things walking around by the sound of twigs cracking. It's amazing how loud it gets in the woods when nobody is talking. I could see the other campfires off in the distance so I kinda thought I wasn't alone, but that didn't last long.

Finally all the campfires had to be put out and it was dark outside. It was a cloudy night, so there were no stars in the sky. I could hear thunder in the distance making its way toward us. It was like a scene out of "Friday the 13th." I had to use my flashlight to see where I was walking, it was so dark.

I made it to my tent and decided I needed to pee before I

went in. No way was I going to get up at night and walk outside to do it, that's for sure. There are monsters in these woods, I thought. Fear was starting to get the best of me. I even got a little panicky as I heard more branches cracking and leaves shuffling. I felt a little sick and didn't know what I should do. We were allowed to blow our whistle for help if something happened, but who wanted to be the baby who blew his whistle?

Not that I didn't come close. I put the whistle in my mouth and almost blew it one time. Then I remembered the conversation Max and I had on our way to Camp Eagle.

He asked me if I was afraid and I told him a little. He told me that it was all right to have fear. Everybody experiences it from time to time. He said, "Joe, when I was in the war, I was scared more than once."

Him, afraid? No way. He was with the airborne unit, and they called him Mad Max. He's like Jet Li—he's not afraid of anything. And that's exactly what I told him. He just laughed.

That's the movies, he said. In real life, men get afraid. Fear is a powerful emotion. Sometimes it makes men totally freeze up. I know what Max was talking about there—I've certainly frozen up my share of times. Stupid bullies. They had me scared all the time. It's so nice not to be a chicken twenty-four hours a day anymore.

Max said you don't always freeze from fear. Some people go into action. We all experience fear, but it's how we react to it that counts. Like with being afraid of rejection when asking a girl out. That fear is real—and don't I know it! But like Max said when Kathy told me no, it's not the fear that's the problem. When you feel fear you have to act on it the right way.

He told me that when I feel fear, I have to ask myself why I'm feeling that way. Is the fear real? In the war he had that feeling and it was a real fear 'cause he could sense something wasn't right in the air. When he felt that, he got himself prepared to take immediate action. But if I feel fear and I can't figure out a real, logical reason to feel it, then I have to look at it for what it is—which is fear of not being in control, or fear of the unknown. That kind of fear can cripple you. And that's the kind of fear I knew I was having in the tent. I mean, what could really hurt me out here? There are a bunch of Boy Scouts all around. There aren't any animals in the woods that would hurt me. The little food I have is outside at the edge of my site. If anything, the bear would take my food, though I might fight him for it because that's all I have. But what else could hurt me?

Thinking about that, I calmed down, took the whistle out of my mouth, and got ready for bed. I crawled into my sleeping bag and cuddled into a ball, telling myself Max has never lied to me, there is nothing out there that can hurt me, and the next thing I knew, it was morning and I was still breathing.

It got only easier the second night. Max is right. He told me that some President said, "The only thing you have to fear is fear itself." I think I understand what that means now.

Tomorrow I'll be done with the first part of the Order of the Arrow. I'm happy I decided to do it and face my fears. I feel a lot better about myself. Now I gotta get some sleep. Even in the woods before I fall asleep I still visualize every night that I'm in a band with my red electric guitar. As always, the audience is clapping and cheering as my band performs. I can see it in my mind, my guitar in my hands, me up on a stage, playing in a band. I am thankful for my chance to perform. It feels great!

Journal Entry 40 - August 14

Hot darn! What an incredible experience today. I made a difference.

Back on Monday, Tom was back in town and gave me a call. He

was just back from baseball camp and wanted to try out his new stuff. He told me that a bunch of kids were trying to get a game going for Thursday. I reminded him what happened a couple of years ago when I blew the game for the team. He told me not to worry about it. "It's only for fun. Come on!" he said. Yeah, I heard that before.

I agreed to go after he kept bugging me about it. I like Tom and I now know that I'm lucky to have him as a friend. Our friendship just sort of happened, and that's how you know you've got a good one. None of that trying to impress stuff. Besides, I was still so proud of having accomplished the Ordeal for the Order of the Arrow. Tom and Danny made it, too. All three of us congratulated each other at the closing ceremony at Camp Eagle. What a threesome! Vinnie was right. We are like the Three Musketeers—all for one and one for all. Maybe I figured that if I could live through the Ordeal, I could live through a baseball game. Anyway, I said I'd play and now Tom was counting on me. I had three days to figure out how to do it without totally humiliating myself.

So I came up with a plan. This time I figured I'd try Max's approach to things. Heck, it worked when I went biking!

The first part of my plan was practice. I needed to practice and as hard as it is to ask Trevor for anything, I decided to see if he'd throw the ball around with me in the backyard. He loves baseball and is very good at it. He's always in the line-up in the town's league.

To my amazement, the little rodent agreed to help. Sort of! It cost me a couple of candy bars and some ice cream but it was worth it. He just can't do anything without taking advantage of anyone. Selfish brat!

Still, it totally helped to throw the ball around with him. I asked him to throw it up like a pop fly so I'd have to run to catch the ball. We practiced a couple of evenings after I got home from work. I was getting better every time. Practice sure makes a difference. I was feeling better about being able to catch the ball even with the little we did.

I could have done without his insults, though. Every time he'd throw the ball up to make me run for it, he'd say something awful. "Run, Yubbie! You call that running? You look like a major league hippo." What he says doesn't even make sense. Did you ever see a hippo trying to catch a baseball? Maybe in the cartoons!

It was the day of the game. All the kids on my team were friendly. No one said anything about the last time we played. I asked if I could play right field and everyone agreed. Again I waited for everyone to choose their batting order and I ended up last.

The game started and it was moving fast. Hit after hit, my team managed to get the bases loaded in the top of the second inning. It was my turn up to bat. I tried not to let those old memories enter my mind, but it was hard. I started getting nervous as I walked up to the plate. I took a deep breath and let it out to try calm myself, but I still was shaking.

The pitcher let go, and I watched the ball come directly at me. I let the bat loose and . . . strike! Uh-oh. The second pitch came—strike two! I took another breath and told myself to relax. The third pitch and CRACK!, I hit the ball. It went right into center field. I couldn't believe it. I ran as fast as I could to first base while a runner scored. Cool!

Unfortunately, the next two batters struck out and the inning was over. When I got to the dugout, Tom shook my hand and said, "Great job, Joe. What a hit." I sat back in amazement. I hit the ball. Wow!

I didn't have as much luck the next three times at bat, but I didn't feel really bad. The other team had a good pitcher who threw the ball fast. Mostly, I think I got too excited about hitting the ball and started swinging kind of crazy. At least I'd hit it once and a runner came in.

It was the top of the ninth and their team was up, with the bases loaded and two outs. My team was ahead by one. Not much of a lead. I was thinking maybe I'd get through the whole game without having to do anything in right field. But then a left-handed batter came up to hit. Lefties are rare, and they usually hit to right field. This was deja vu—the last time, when I tripped and lost the game, it was a leftie who hit it my way.

I started to panic but remembered Max's words. I started to focus on breathing in and exhaling all the air out. The first pitch—strike one. Good, I thought, we're almost there. Second pitch—strike two. Oh, man, I don't have to worry. One more strike and the game is over. Third pitch—CRACK!—the ball went flying into the air in my direction. Just like I'd been picturing in my head all week, I focused on the ball as it flew in the air, running as fast as I could toward it. I could see it coming down as I was closing in. I ran harder and faster. It was coming in as I reached out my glove . . . and tripped. Wouldn't you know it? I got totally airborne, like Superman, only close to the ground and ready to eat serious turf. Thing is, the ball landed smack in my glove as I fell through the air. I caught it! I hit the ground hard but managed to keep the ball in my glove. I jumped up showing everybody that I had the ball and my whole dugout came running onto the field. It was crazy! The first kid jumped on me and I fell down and everybody else jumped on top.

I made a difference today, and it was because of Max and his brain whammy stuff. My most important tool did the job. His key has opened up new doors for me. I sit here writing in my journal feeling so much different this time around. I couldn't help flipping back in my journal to the entry about the game two years ago. How pathetic I was back then. The answer was with me all the time.

I'm off to bed now, right after I practice some on my red electric guitar. I still keep visualizing every night that I'm in a band with my guitar. I still see the audience clapping and cheering as my band performs. It still feels great to be up on the stage. I still see it all in my mind, my guitar in my hands, me up on a stage playing in a band. Now I know for sure that if I can see it in my mind, I can make it happen in real life.

Journal Entry 41 - August 30

My heart has been ripped out, cut into small pieces, and served to Hannibal Lector for supper.

I can't believe what happened tonight. I should have known better. I can't trust Trevor. He's such a liar, a no good thief, and now he's done the unthinkable.

About mid-summer, after talking to Max, I decided to take my chances and ask a girl on a date. Her name is Jane. She's a knockout.

I was at Anthony's Pool. I wasn't going to have many chances this summer to go and spend time swimming. Between working in the afternoons and all the activities I have with the Boy Scouts, my summer is pretty filled up.

I wasn't afraid any more to go there and swim. If someone was going to pick on me, I was going straight over to Mr. Anthony and tell him what happened. Max told me one day that there's a difference between tattling and telling. Tattling is when you're trying to hurt someone and telling is when you want to protect someone. I'll never forget the difference, and I'm not afraid of telling an adult anymore. Shoot, look what happened to Hank!

I walked right up to Jane with two sodas in my hand and said, "I bought this for you. Can I sit down?" She looked at me and smiled and then said, "Okay." One word, but it totally made my day. I swear, Max is the man with the plan that always tells me that I can. Cool!

Jane was very nice to talk to. I had a great time making her laugh all afternoon. When she had to leave, she said, "I like you, Joe. You're really a funny guy." I asked her for her phone number and the romance began.

I started calling her and we had some great talks. We were supposed to meet at Anthony's again for the afternoon. Then the weirdest thing happened. Trevor asked if he could walk with me to Anthony's. This was very strange. All of a sudden he wants to hang? I asked him what was up and he just said that he was going that way so why not go together. Wrong! I know better then to believe whatever Trevor says.

I asked Trevor again as we started walking down the street. What's up? I know he's not trying to become buds. He told me that he tried to get back into Anthony's and Mr. Anthony told him that he wasn't going to tolerate his behavior and he wasn't going allow him to come back.

Trevor thought that if I was with him and asked Mr. Anthony to let him back in, because I was Mr. A's pet, then maybe he could get back in. That sounded more like Trevor—sneaky and shifty. I thought about telling him to beat it, but then I thought about Max. I bet he'd tell me to give Trevor a chance. I agreed to talk to Mr. Anthony, but only if Trevor swore he'd be good. What did we have to lose? If Mr. Anthony said no, it was no skin off my nose. Trevor could walk home by himself.

To my surprise, Mr. Anthony said, "If Trevor promises never to pull a stunt again I will let him back." Trevor shook his head and agreed.

"Alright," I told Trevor, "you're back. Now leave me alone. I have to go and see someone." He said okay and walked off.

My timing was good, because Jane was coming in the front gate. I walked over to her and said hi. We picked up a couple of sodas and went off to sit at a picnic table to talk.

All of a sudden Trevor shows up at the table. I got a real bad feeling about it. "What do you want?" I asked. Then he started in with how there wasn't anybody there he knew, and how he figured he'd talk to me and "this pretty girl." Red alert! Something was up.

I told Trevor flat-out to leave me alone, but Jane said, "No, that's okay, Joe. He's cute. Let him stay." What was I supposed to do? I'd hardly call Trevor cute. But then, I know him enough to see him on the inside, like Max says. Trevor's stupid deep, dark tan and Mr. Macho body may make girls like him, but I know better.

The whole afternoon went terrible. Jane is one year younger than me and Trevor is two years. When I talked, he talked and then she talked. It was very hard to have a personal conversation with Jane while Trevor was breathing down my neck. But I didn't know how to get him to leave. He spent all afternoon with us. I hate that kid.

It was time to leave, and not too soon as far as I was concerned. I just wanted to get him away from Jane. On the way home I chewed him out, telling him to leave me alone when I'm with a girl. It wasn't my fault that he couldn't find someone to hang with. He should have just gone home or done what I've done so many times and taken a roll of quarters and played video games or pinball all afternoon.

Then the jerk actually said, "But Jane is way better to look at than some video game screen."

Whoa! I saw red, big time. I told him to get his own girlfriend. He never has a problem finding some girl to go ga-ga over him. But he laughed and said, "What, are you jealous, Fatso? Yubbie can't get a date?"

I started chewing him out more, but he just took off. I figured he'd had his fun tormenting me and thought that was the end of it.

Because of work and Boy Scouts, I only go to Anthony's once a week. So I didn't get to see Jane at Anthony's again until today. I talk to her on the phone several times a week, but seeing her is way better. We had a great time. She told me that her parents were going out tonight and said I could come over her house if I wanted. Wow! I've died and gone to heaven! Of course I said yes.

After supper I did my chores and told Ma that I was going out. Dad was already in the living room watching TV and wouldn't notice if I was home or not. I didn't actually tell Ma where I was going, though, just "out." That was good enough for her. She told me I had to be back by 9:30 and then headed into the living room to join Dad.

9:30. No problem. As I walked out the door Trevor asked me where I was going. Like I'd tell him. "None of your business," I said. Apparently that was the wrong thing, though, because it made him more interested. Now he wanted to go with me. I swear, that twerp can't let me have anything of my own going on.

"There's no way you're going with me to Jane's house," I snapped. Second dumb thing to say. He immediately said, "I definitely want to go now."

It didn't matter to him when I pointed out that she's my girlfriend, not his. He started in on the threats, saying that if I didn't take him, he'd tell Dad that I went over to a girl's house when her parents weren't home. He didn't even have to explain. I knew that Dad would kick my butt if he knew. I tried to bribe Trevor with money, but no luck. He was going no matter what.

What was I going to do now? Jane was expecting me. Finally I said, "Okay, but I want some time alone with her so we can talk." He got this innocent look on his face and promised to sit and watch TV so we could "do whatever." Man, I wanted to beat the snot out of him. I could tell he was going to ruin this for me.

Jane was cool about Trevor showing up with me. She let us in and invited us to sit in the den. Not what I had in mind. Trevor had promised to take a hike to the living room when we got there. We all sat down and to my amazement a conversation broke out. I asked if Jane and I could go somewhere and talk. Jane said, "Well, that would be kinda rude to Trevor, Joe. He walked across town, too, and I don't imagine it was to watch TV." That sounded weird to me.

We sat around and talked until it was time to leave. My night had been ruined and I was thinking of how many ways I was going to beat up Trevor on the way home. I was so mad.

As we were walking down her walkway, Trevor said, "Oops, I forgot my hat. Wait here and I'll be right back." I was standing there, thinking about how upset I was by what he did to me, when I suddenly realized that he still hadn't come back. It had been ten minutes already, at least. I walked toward the house and peeked in the front picture window. It was awful! There they were, Jane and Trevor, talking and laughing next to the couch. Jane was touching Trevor's arm. It was so obvious. They *liked* each other! I couldn't believe my eyes. My heart fell down to my feet and it tried to get out of my little toe, dig a hole in the earth, and jump in.

How? Why? It doesn't matter. Jane has crushed me. I'm mad at Trevor, but I really couldn't understand why Jane would do that to me. I had to walk home without Trevor, knowing Jane wants him and not me. What a crummy night! I tried to give a girl my heart and she stomped it to death.

Just now Trevor came to my room. He acted all innocent. "Why didn't you wait?" he said.

"You know why, Trevor. You just stole my girlfriend."

He smiled, like he was glad I saw. Or like he was proud or something. "That's tough, Yubbie. The handsomer guy won. We're going steady." I told him to leave me alone.

Tonight sucked. This pain sucks. I want it gone.

I'm not really in the mood to visualize being in a band tonight. But I know I should. I have to, if I want it to happen in real life. I have to see myself in a band with my red electric guitar. I have to see the audience clapping and cheering as my band performs. It have to feel how great it is to be up on the stage. And maybe then, for a few minutes at least, I won't feel like the world just bashed me over the head with a red electric guitar.

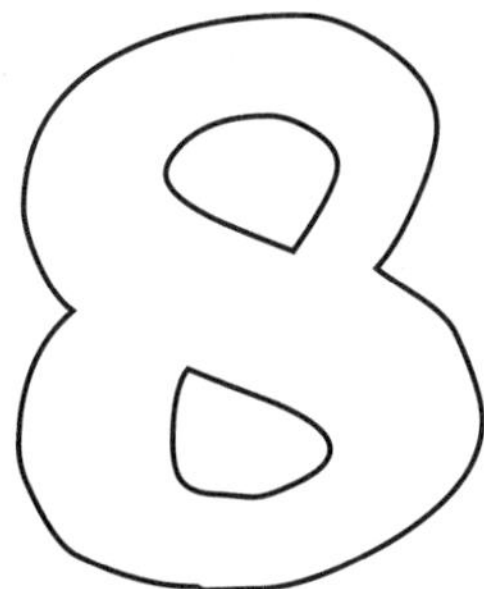

Journal Entry 42 - September 12

It's Saturday—delivery day at the store. Even though it's been several days since the whole Trevor and Jane thing, I'm still stewing about it. Max sensed that right away. He asked me what's up and I laid it out, fast and furious. I told him what Trevor did, and how much I hate Trevor, and how that hate boils inside me all the time. I just want to kill my brother.

I don't feel too swell about Jane, either. I want to go over to her house and call her words that I can't even write down. It would be like you see on TV when they blip out swearing. @#$%^&*!@#$%^&*!@#$%^&. My blip would be so long that it would wrap around the planet twenty thousand times. I still can't believe she did that to me.

Max was, as usual, real calm about the whole thing. He said he was sorry that I had to experience the betrayal of both my brother and girlfriend. He told me to turn it into an opportunity to learn about human behavior. Here I'm thinking about killing someone and he's talking about education. He sure can be confusing.

He went on to explain that it's hard sometimes to understand and accept peoples' actions. He knew I was very upset and angry. Gee, was it the "I want to kill him" line that clued him in? As mad as I was, I had to bite my tongue not to say anything mean to Max. He didn't do anything.

Max talked about hatred. He called it a poison as deadly as anthrax. Once the poison gets into our blood, it spreads throughout every organ in our body and begins to destroy every cell. It eats you from the inside out. He was right about that. Here he was, trying to help me, and all I could think about was punching him or anyone else who'd come close enough. I just wanted to hit something, anything!

The sad part about it, he said, is that the person who hurts you doesn't even know about the pain you're experiencing. Which is exactly why I want to kill Trevor slowly—I'm going to torture him first so he can understand my pain, and then I'll put him out of his misery.

Max didn't act all shocked when I told him that. He just said, "Well, even though that might work, the consequence that you'd have to pay is too high." Party pooper. But I have to admit, it made me stop a second. I don't want to have to go to jail. And I suppose I don't really want to kill Trevor. I just want him to suffer somehow, to feel some of the pain he heaped on me.

Then I remembered Max's background. My talk about killing someone might hit too close to home. I tried to start breathing deeply, to calm down. It helped a little.

He told me to remember that people are just people, with all their strengths and weaknesses, just like me. I have to accept that, just as much as I have to accept my own strengths and weaknesses. The poison of hatred can destroy you, he said, if you don't learn to let it go and to forgive people for just being human. By hating people who hurt us, we give them the power to steal away our happiness. He said I had to forgive them.

Me? I had to forgive them? Neither one of them even apologized!

"Anger and forgiveness can't exist at the same time," Max said. I could pick one, and one only. He recommended forgiveness, of course. "Joe, you are doing it for you, not them. It's the poison that has invaded your being and is disturbing your peaceful state that has to leave. That's why you do it. So it leaves you and you can go back to being happy."

I guess he was right. I haven't felt even close to happy since this happened. Still, something was missing: Trevor and Jane were getting away with hurting me. Don't they have to pay some kind of price?

That's where Max mentioned some big names. Buddhism and Taoism. Big time philosophies. He's studied those and a bunch of others. He took what he felt he could use to be a better man and understand his existence and how he connects to the world around him. His studies taught him about something called Karma. That means, what you put out in life is what you get back. So because of Karma, I don't have to get back at Trevor and Jane for doing something that hurt me. Their actions will at eventually come back to them, and then, basically, they'll "get theirs."

The flip side of that is, what I do will come back to me. Hello! I better not be killing anybody then!

So I guess I've decided to forgive Trevor and Jane. It ain't easy, that's for sure. Max sounds like he knows what he's talking about, but that's not the way I'm used to doing things. Please tell me this will get easier the more I practice.

Journal Entry 43 - September 29

The Avenger has struck and they'll think twice about doing me wrong again! The caped marvel came down from the heavens and foiled the evildoers' plan. With fire in his eyes and electricity bolting out his fingertips, he found the bad guys and destroyed them in their plot. The bullies didn't get away with it this time.

I was walking home today from school when I noticed a bunch of kids picking on this little kid across the street. The little guy looked very nerdy, with large, black, squared glasses, a book bag bulging at the seams, and walking like the hunchback of Notre Dame under the sheer weight of it. It looked like he was carrying the world on this back.

Five much older kids were picking on him. It was like a scene out of my past. I got angry real fast. As I picked up speed, I was hoping to get to the store across the street from where they were taunting this kid and get help. I walked by a group of other kids on my side of the street, just watching.

I banged into two of them and couldn't help but snap out, "Are you just going to stand there and look stupid?" I think that shocked them. As I made my way through their group I was furious. The whole thing brought back memories of Vinnie. I couldn't let this continue. I knew I had to do something about it. I knew that it was my responsibility to help this kid in need. I considered busting over there myself. I know I'm getting older and I'm getting bigger and sometimes I think that's a good thing. Heck, I'm in eighth grade getting ready for high school, and I tip the scales at 240 pounds. Sometimes I feel like I could run through a wall or jump up and come smashing down on someone if they tried to pick on me now. I have no intention of letting anyone get away with anything anymore.

But I haven't gone through what I've gone through with Hank and Max and Trevor and all that Karma business without smarting up. Crushing those guys across the street wouldn't be the answer, even if I could've pulled it off. I darted into the store and told the man behind the register to call the police and get help for the kid being tormented across the street. By now they were slapping him around. The man dialed 911. After he reported it to the police station and hung up, I asked him to go help the little kid. I almost said "Yikes!" out loud when I saw him come from behind the register with a baseball bat. He was the one who'd get arrested if he started swinging that thing!

I think he was just trying to look tough, though. He stormed outside holding the bat and screaming, "Hey, leave that kid alone! I just called the cops and they'll be here any minute." Just as fast as the shutter of a camera blinks, the bullies stopped what they were doing, looked at the angry storekeeper, and took off running down the street and ducking down an alleyway.

The little kid was on his knees picking up his books and putting them back in his bag. I went over to talk to him. I told him my name was Joe and asked him for his. "Leroy," he said. He had tears in his eyes. The poor kid. I've been there, so I know.

I helped him pick up his books and told him it was all right and that I understood. He looked at me, all surprised. "I'll bet nobody ever picks on you," he says. "You're so big." Man, was that how he saw me? Like some big tough guy? That's a first. I told him I was picked on a lot when I was his age. I asked him if he wanted me to walk him home. He nodded, and I walked him to the bottom of his street.

I felt really good helping him. I know I still haven't figured it all out yet, but I did understand how it felt to be him. I wasn't going to let anyone touch him while I was with him. Heck, I'm Big Tough Guy! What a laugh.

I told Leroy that I walk home this way on Tuesdays and Thursdays and would be happy to walk with him anytime. He said thanks, smiled, and walked up the street.

I was proud of myself. I walked home and wanted to tell someone what I did. I called Max at the store. He said he was impressed with my action and my desire to help someone else in trouble. He called it the desire to intervene. That Max, he has some doozies.

Max explained that I'd stepped up and taken action, and that most people won't do that. They don't want to get involved. The story of my life! Well, until I met Max. I guess he has a desire to intervene, too.

Then Max said he was proud of me. Wow! I got all teary-eyed and felt a chill going down my back when he said that. It feels so good. He makes me feel special.

What a day this turned out to be. On top of sticking up for that little kid, I heard a couple of kids at school talking about getting together to practice as a band. Ron and Jeff are their names. I know them from math class. I told them that I had an electric guitar and that I could play it. I wasn't even bragging this time—I really can play it! It turns out Ron plays base guitar and Jeff plays drums. Perfect! We all agreed just to get together and jam. We made plans for later this week. That is so cool! I couldn't believe it. I'm so close to getting in a band. Maybe Max was right. It's all in my head.

So of course tonight I'm going to visualize being in a band with my red electric guitar like I've never pictured it before. I'm going to visualize it LOUD. I'll see the audience clapping and cheering LOUD as my band performs LOUD. It'll feel great to be up on the stage. I'll see my guitar in my hands. And this time, I'll be playing it with Ron and Jeff. Cool!

Journal Entry 44 - December 2

Max was right again. Trevor got his. He got snagged, big time. Finally, Karma bit him right in the butt for all the means things he has ever done—to me and anyone else. My brother is on his way out.

Ever since Trevor stole Jane away from me, I avoid him like the plague. He's just mean all over. He doesn't even go out with Jane anymore after she caught him kissing another girl at the movie theater. Well, I guess she got hers, too. I didn't have to do a thing. It's that Karma stuff, I know. Now Jane knows what it feels like when someone goes behind your back and cheats on you. I don't wish anyone pain—at least that's the way Max tells me I should think and I'm really trying to—but it's hard not to enjoy their big Karma Kick in the Pants. Maybe someday I can think like Max, just not quite yet.

Trevor had been picking on a kid at his school, or so I heard when Ma was trying to explain what happened to one of her friends on the phone. The principal told Ma that Trevor had gotten a bunch of detentions for making "disturbances" in the classroom and pushing this kid around during recess.

Ma said that the principal had called her up several times before to speak to her about Trevor. She told her friend, "I told that principal that my Trevor would never do anything like that. He's a good kid." I laid on the couch listening to her conversation almost busting my gut laughing. Trevor would never do that? Give me a break! Trevor is a monster hiding in sheep's clothing. He's like the trapdoor spider waiting to attack the poor victim as it passes by its camouflaged hinged silk door, waiting for the vibrations of its target and then—BAM-O! Dead target.

Well, this time it doesn't matter what Ma tells the principal, there ain't no getting away with it. Several students saw Trevor punch the kid in the chest. What Trevor didn't know was that the kid was sick with some kind of medical problem, and that punch really hurt him. The kid was rushed off to the hospital in an ambulance.

Ma had to go to the school and so did the police. They took Trevor to the police station. I couldn't believe it. He got a ride in a police car, but it wasn't in the front seat playing with all the sirens and flashing lights.

Ma had to call Dad at work. He rushed home and picked Ma up. He was mad—double mad. Veins were bulging out of his forehead. Seriously, he was scary. I tried to blend into the woodwork. I didn't want to accidentally get in his way or anything. He was yelling at Ma as they walked out the door to go to the station. I had a feeling Trevor would be glad to be behind bars when Dad got there. I remember thinking that the cops better have some really big sticks out because they'd have to beat Dad back from his own kid, that's for darn sure.

Ma told her friend on the phone that when Dad arrived at the station, he went ballistic and started screaming at the police. They told him to calm down or they'd put handcuffs on him. Man! If I could've been a fly on the wall for THAT. The Torture Chamber Master met his match.

The police decided to keep Trevor and called Social Services. The lieutenant told Ma and Dad that they had to wait for the kid's parents to come down to the police station to see if they were pressing charges. The fact that the kid was in the hospital made the police think that Trevor would be charged with assault and battery. They also told Ma and Dad that they better hope nothing more happens to the kid or the district attorney might file more serious charges.

Dad went off the deep end. Ma said he just kept walking back and forth yelling. He couldn't wait to get his hands on Trevor. The police kept warning Dad to relax. Finally, they brought him into the room with Trevor. The first thing Dad did was slap Trevor in the back of the head. I guess the police told him that if he did that once more they'd arrest him for child abuse. Dad didn't take it lightly, and he told them that Trevor was his kid and that he paid their salary. Yeah, that was a smart thing to tell the police.

The head cop came down to the detention room and talked to Dad. I would LOVE to know what the guy said, because according to Ma, Dad calmed down and actually listened.

Not that he was calm when he got home. I'm no dummy, I was upstairs. Outta sight, outta hitting distance! Dad's a lunatic when he's mad. I could hear him upstairs as Ma told him to stop yelling. He kept yelling at her to leave him alone. I started wondering if his belt was for Ma, too, and that freaked me out. I sat down behind my bedroom door, wondering what I'd do if that happened. But it didn't. Eventually Ma told him to leave the house and he did. I think the front door is broken from his slamming it so hard.

That's when I came downstairs and Ma called her girlfriend.

Wow! Talk about a hurricane. What an explosion hit our house! Ma was crying, Dad split to who knows where, and Trevor is locked up.

I wonder if that's where Trevor gets his anger from—the Torture Chamber Master? When Max talked about how bullies have problems at home or they see violence around them and act out, he was talking about my house. But me, I'm not like that. I don't get mean. I've always been the chicken that shivered in the corner and never struck back. If Max is right, Trevor is the result of what has happened to him just like I'm the result of what has happened to me. And now I'm thinking that maybe being a chicken wasn't a bad thing. For once I'm glad to have been Yubbie. I never want to be like Dad, Ma, Trevor, or Randy. I want to be like Max. He'd never yell and go off like Dad. Max tries to be relaxed. He says when he feels upset or something, he takes deep breaths to calm down. And he tells himself that he's happy, so he is happy. He even stayed happy after I told him I broke the handmade medal presentation case that some general gave him. Dad would've ripped my head off.

It's almost time to go to bed. I was happy about one thing today. I talked to Ron and Jeff. We've been having a lot of fun jamming and now they have two more kids who want to play with us. John plays the keyboard and Bill plays guitar. It's starting to come together! We're trying to practice twice a week at Ron's house. His dad lets us set up in the garage to wail out some tunes.

I can see it now. I'm in a band with my red electric guitar. I see the audience clapping and cheering as we perform. It feels great to be up on the stage. My guitar is in my hands. I'm playing a song with Ron, Jeff, John, and Bill. I can smell the air in the auditorium, feel the electricity of the crowd, and I'm thankful for my chance to perform. It feels great! The announcer's voice comes on and introduces us as....

Hey! We need a name! How could I have forgotten that? I'll have to give this some thought.

I want to think about so many things and draw them to me like a magnet, not just my band. I'd like to see myself in a family where everyone is laughing as they all sit at the kitchen table having supper. I'd like to see my dad come home and pat me on the head and tell me that he loves me. Yeah, I'd like to see that, as impossible as it sounds.

Journal Entry 45 - February 29

Things have finally calmed down at the house. The daily yelling has slowed down ever since a judge found Trevor guilty of assault and battery charges. Because the kid he hit was so majorly injured, and because Dad has such a bad temper, the judge sent Trevor to a detention facility. He has to stay there for ninety days. I really hope he gets help. And I really hope he'll stay longer. It's nice not having him around.

I know I shouldn't think that way. I mean, all this is serious stuff. But him being gone is like having a thorn taken out of my side. That continuous stabbing pain that gnawed at me every day is gone.

Because Dad lost his temper in court and yelled at the judge, he's got to take some anger classes to learn how to calm down. I hope this helps him and he becomes easier to live with. I haven't seen anything different about him yet—but then, I haven't been ticking him off. I stay far away from him these days.

I've been keeping Max informed about everything. He was happy to hear that Trevor is getting some help and that Dad is taking those classes. He told me that he thinks that my dad is holding some really bad feelings inside and with the classes maybe he will let them out or at least realize that they're there and not act so violently when he gets upset.

It makes sense to me when Max talks about emotions we hold inside. He says that hatred, anger, and bitterness in life are like the core of the earth. It's like molten lava building up pressure. When there's the slightest crack in the earth, like when something upsets Dad, the pressure finds a way out and explodes into the air. That's one of the reasons Max meditates. He tells me that it keeps him cool and calm because he's in touch with his inner self. I'm not clear about that but I'll take his word.

Instead of molten lava, he believes that there's a lake with cool water in him that is soothing and relaxing. There's no pressure and that's why he doesn't get upset. He says, "I put things into perspective."

That's a hard one for me to understand. He said he kinda analyzes every situation that comes up and decides if he should react to it or not. He thinks before he reacts. And he says that when he looks at the big picture of life, sometimes it isn't worth the energy to get upset. He just accepts it and lets it go like the mist of an ocean wave brushing his face as it crashes into the rocks below. He sure has a different way of looking at things. I don't know if I buy it all, but when I see my dad and I see Max, I tend to think that Max is better off with his deep thinking.

We went out to make deliveries today. I told Max that I really don't want to be like my dad and work in a factory for the rest of my life making roller chain. He's so unhappy. Maybe that's why he has so much molten lava inside. Max laughed and said he thinks there are many things responsible for my dad's boiling lava.

Max says that every one of us is given a special talent by the nature of our existence. And that we also have a purpose. We have to take the time to discover both. Some people find their talents early in life, like many musicians and artists. Most of us, he said, have to keep trying different things until we find what gives us great happiness. That's the key, he said. Most people don't like their jobs. They never find out what their special talents are and so they don't use those talents to earn a living. If they did, they'd be so much happier and find it so much easier to go to work every day.

I don't want to work in Dad's factory. I want to find out what talents nature gave me so that I can choose a job I like.

Max said that we have to try different things like sports, art, and other things to find out what our talent is. It may take many years, so it's important to be patient. In time we make the discovery. He says that it could be around one of the subjects that we do well in at school. In my case, my desire to play in a band may mean that music is my special talent. We have to try and see where it takes us.

We don't have to earn a living with our special talent, but it's lucky if we can. Max told me that it took many years for him to find his talent. He thought that being a soldier in the military was his talent but later discovered that it was his ability to create a plan, organize the necessary things, and then follow them through to the end. That's how come he runs a business so well. He also knows that part of his talent is talking to people and helping others accomplish important things. His special talent and his purpose kinda go hand in hand. That's neat.

He made me think of Mary Lou. I think she was right when she said maybe because I've felt so much pain in my life and it has made me very sensitive to others feeling pain, that my special talent is helping people. Like Max does. Maybe that's why I met Max. You never know. Maybe, just maybe, he's my teacher. I changed the way I look at things because of all the conversations we've had. Is that his job? Helping kids like me change the way we think? He doesn't get paid for it, but he tells me that his store is very successful and he makes a good living.

He says that he considers himself a very rich man. Not only does he have his store, but he also has a bunch of friends and people in his life. They all make him feel special and that makes him real happy.

I told Max today that I've been thinking about all the stuff he keeps telling me. I've decided not to be so mad at my Dad anymore and to try to understand that he has the problem and not me. I will definitely try to avoid upsetting him so I don't get a beating. Same with Ma. I think she needs help, too. I don't know what happened in their lives to make them that way, and maybe it's not important for me to know the why. What is important is to just accept them like they are and know that's the way they've decided to be. Me, I'm going to be different. I'm going be happy and become what I want: Famous!

Bedtime is here. I'm not going to stop with visualizing the band this time. When I'm done with the band, I'm planning to lay quietly looking inside me. I hope I can see that very special talent. Who knows, maybe it'll stand up and wave and I'll find it early on. Wouldn't that be cool?

Journal Entry 46 - April 1

This ain't no April Fool—Yubbie and His Crusaders exists!

Tonight was the best night EVER. Yubbie and His Crusaders got a standing ovation and won first place in the junior high talent contest.

It started when the five of us decided to get together to jam. I told the group that I'd wanted to form a band for a long time. It was amazing how we worked together. There wasn't any fighting or arguing. Everyone was up for learning a few songs. Then, during one of our breaks, I mentioned that our school was having a talent contest at the beginning of April, and if we could learn one song really well, we could give it a shot. Everyone agreed. We still hadn't decided what to call ourselves.

We started practicing five nights a week. Each of us picked a song that we'd like to play, and after a couple of weeks of practice, we chose one that we all agreed we played best. That's the one we played at the talent show. Everyone was happy with the choice.

The name was harder. No, we didn't fight about it or anything. It was just tough to come up with the right one. We thought of Down Under, and The Cruisers, and Down Easy, and Blitz. But none of them sounded right. We kept thinking on it and tried to focus on the music for a while.

Like Max always tells me, you have to have a plan, organize it, and follow through. That's what I did. I got everyone to agree that we needed to practice five days a week and made sure that at the end of each practice I reminded everyone of our goal. I even turned it into a jingle. It went like this, "Five guys practicing five nights a week to perform five perfect minutes to receive five perfect grades from our judges."

After a couple of nights, I had everyone repeating the jingle. Every week Max would ask me how things were going and I'd give him an update. He'd remind me to keep focused, to see that big night in my mind every night before I went to bed, and to make sure I didn't boss the guys around but instead helped them to understand that we were a team and everyone had to hold up their end of the deal.

Last week at one of our breaks I threw out my thoughts of a name. I told the guys that we were like crusaders—kids who were on a mission to succeed. Max really has been rubbing off on me. I told them that's what we should call ourselves—Crusaders. They liked the Crusaders in part because we all agreed that we had been working real hard. Ron kiddingly said, "Hey, let's call it Yubbie and His Crusaders," knowing that I get a little irritated with my old nickname. He knows he can get away with it because we're good friends and I know he would never do anything to hurt me. Both of us like to kid around with each other, and I know if one of us felt offended we could be honest enough to call the other guy on it.

I looked at him all fake mad. Everyone laughed—not at the name, but more at the way I looked at Ron, like I was going to take his bass guitar and stick it where the sun don't shine. Ron got this funny smile, like he was thinking real hard and liking what he thought, "Think of it, Joe. When we get famous and we're performing at the Coliseum, you can get up there and tell all the girls, Yubbie, Yubbie, I got luvvvvv all around me. They're gonna give you all kinds of lovin'."

Now it was my turn to get a funny smile. I remembered back to a conversation I had with Max. He said I have the power to make something painful or not. That nickname would only define me if I let it define me.

That was it. A name I hated so much, a name that made me cry so many times, and I was now going to use it to define me—but on my terms. I'm a hefty 230 pounds and why hide it? Why not use it instead? Cool!

Everyone agreed to call the group Yubbie and His Crusaders.

The talent show was only a week away and we felt we were ready. I asked Ma if she and Dad were going. She told me that she wouldn't miss it for anything. She told me that my dad said, "Well, you know how much I hate going out after a long day of work."

"I'll keep bugging him and maybe he'll show up," Ma said. Not likely, but if she wanted to try, fine. I wasn't going to let it hurt me if he didn't. Max has really helped me learn to accept Dad just the way he is. If he can't tell me that he loves me or he can't make it to my performance, it's not a reflection on me as a person. It's a reflection of who he is and he has to deal with it, not me.

I told Max that I had an extra ticket and wondered if he would attend. He said, "Did Moses let the Red Sea stop him? Joe, I can't wait. Wild horses couldn't keep me away." He cracks me up. I told him about the name we chose and he shook his head and said, "You have gained great insight, grasshopper," and bowed to me. I bowed back in respect.

It was the big night. There were people all over the place. The school cafeteria was jam-packed. I listened as each student got up on the stage and performed. I looked out in the audience and saw Ma sitting by herself and felt happy that she'd made it. I scanned the crowd and noticed Max in his black leather jacket. He was hard to miss—his bald head reflected the cafeteria lights. He's really a tough-looking guy. He walks like he's ready to take on the world with his big horseshoe style mustache. But I know he's really about what's on the inside—and there's nothing big and tough about Max on the inside. He's the nicest man ever. It's hard to believe all the bad things that happened to him made him so smart.

Our turn was coming closer and closer. I felt nauseated and scared. And my stomach started growling! I couldn't help but remember that time I was in grammar school and hid in the bathroom so I wouldn't have to get on the stage. Those fears came up like it was only yesterday, and for a second I froze, thinking that I couldn't do it. I felt tightness in my chest and the blood leaving my face. Ron poked me and asked, "Yo, you alright?" I couldn't tell him about my past or what I was feeling.

Then I remembered what Max said about breathing. I started to take in deep breaths and let them out slowly and controlled all the way down to my belly button. As I continued breathing slowly I could feel the nervousness going away. Fear is natural. What I do with it is what determines whether it controls me or not.

With that last thought I could hear the announcer say, "And a new group is here to perform for you tonight. Please help me welcome Yubbie and His Crusaders." The audience started clapping. We ran on stage and picked up our instruments. With a one, two, three, we cranked out our song. Everyone was in beat and at their best.

What a night! After the song, the crowd exploded. I could see Max jump to his feet, applauding. Everyone in the audience joined in as they started to whistle and yell out, "Encore!" Wow! We did it!

I'm so happy. It was exactly the way I visualized it. I was standing on stage holding my red electric guitar. I saw the audience clapping and cheering as I performed. It felt great to be up on the stage. Ron, Jeff, John, Bill, and I played our song. I could smell the air in the auditorium. I could feel the electricity of the crowd. And I was thankful for my chance to perform. We all bowed and left the stage.

While we were in back, we all hugged each other, telling each other how great we were. We were so proud that it came off so well. Then we heard the announcer say, "Wow! It's unanimous. The judges have overwhelmingly chosen Yubbie and His Crusaders as the winners." It was like the speaker shut off. I couldn't hear a thing but my own thoughts. We did it! We did it! Five guys practiced five nights a week to perform five perfect minutes to receive five perfect grades from our judges. We did it!

We all ran out behind the curtain to see our parents. People were patting me on the back, telling me how great it was. I made my way through the crowd. I could see my ma standing with tears in her eyes. I went to her and she hugged me, telling me how proud she was of me and how much she wished that Dad was there to see my performance. Her hug felt so good. I told her I had to see someone and would be right back.

I could see a sparkling bald head making its way toward me. I ran up to Max and gave him a big hug. He patted me on the back and told me what an outstanding job I did and that I should be very proud of my accomplishment. He said that me being happy made him happy.

I don't even remember how I got home. It was all a blur. I was getting ready for bed and had started to write in my journal. There was a knock on my door and a voice on the other side said, "Joe, it's Dad. Are you asleep?" The pen froze in my hand. I wondered what I'd done now? I'd been working so hard to keep my distance from Dad. Was the Torture Chamber Master in need of venting some of his built up anger?

I hid my journal and let him in. He didn't look mad. He said, "Your mother said you did a great job tonight." He flapped his hand toward my guitar, kind of pointing at it. "I wish I'd been there to see it."

I wasn't sure what to say to that. I wished he'd been there, too. He turned and started to go but then he stopped and looked at me. "I just wanted to let you know that I'm proud of you."

Tears started to fill my eyes. I said thanks but I don't know if he heard me. He closed the door and I started balling. It was the first time in my life that Dad ever said he was proud of me.

So maybe it's true, maybe he can change. Maybe I should let

him meet Max and they could go fishing together. Then Dad would listen to him and things would be different.

After Dad left my room, I pulled out this journal again. I couldn't help but flip back through the pages I'd written on. So much has happened since I started this thing. And now there's only a couple of pages to fill up with new stuff. Looking at this journal and thinking about everything I've done, and remembering all my visualizing about how I want things to be and then having those things happen exactly the way I visualized them—well, it makes me think maybe I can change some things that are happening right now. Things I didn't used to think I could change. It makes me want to buy a brand new journal and start imagining something more than just me and the guys on stage with our band.

I see it now—I'm on a stage after my performance and the crowd is going ballistic, yelling and screaming and doing all kinds of crazy things. I walk back stage and I see my ma and dad holding hands, waiting for me to go back to my dressing room. As I approach them, my dad walks toward me and gives me a hug. He whispers in my ear, "I love you, son." I hug him with all my might because that's all I ever wanted to hear. It's like the sound of a perfect note. It's as gentle as the mist of a wave touching my face as it hits the rocks below. It's as soft as a butterfly landing on my nose. I can feel it now.

Epilogue

To Whoever Reads This Journal:

I took a hike today and climbed Mt. Washington in New Hampshire, some 6,200 feet. It's a mountain where a 231-mile wind was recorded in 1934 and that still stands as the world record. I sat on top looking at the majestic beauty in front of me. It took thousands and thousands of years to form this mountain. It wasn't made in a day.

I sit and think back about my life so far. I'm almost eighteen, and sometimes I feel like I've lived a long time. I'm getting ready to go off to college. I'm almost a man. Life has dealt me an unusual hand, that's for sure. I was born into a house with parents who simply weren't suited by nature or nurture to parent. They were disconnected, wrapped up in their own problems, and not tuned in to what was happening with my brothers or me. They were abusive. I had to recognize this, deal with it, and accept that their treatment of me came from who they are, not from who I am, so that I could forgive them and move forward.

I breathe the air of the mountains and it is fresh, clean and pure like the water in the rivers that bubble from its springs, feeding its inhabitants. In the presence of Mt. Washington I sense the strength of all those great presidents who have become a part of its imposing nature in the naming of adjacent mountains: Mount Madison, Mount John Adams, Mount John Quincy Adams, Mount Jefferson, Mount Monroe, Mount Eisenhower, and Mount Pierce. The splendor of these mountains stands strong and bold, even as they show no mercy to anyone who doesn't understand their nature. Such can be life, I think.

In nature there's a point where regular trees have a hard time growing. It's called "the tree line." It's about 4,500 feet above sea level. Past that, it's almost impossible for a healthy tree to exist. I feel like one of the tenacious low spruce or scrub pines above the tree line that have braved the ruthless, torturous, brutal winds that decimate the weak. I've survived above the tree line of life, though there was a price to pay.

I've grown strong in spite of the elements. My exterior is rugged to protect my fragile core, my bark is thick to withstand the inclement weather, my branches are scarce but strong, and my needles short and broad. I may not be the prettiest tree to observe. But my roots are well grounded and cling to the heavy granite so the treacherous winds can't blow me away. I've made it this far, who knows what else I can accomplish?

I learned early that life isn't always easy. It's not always fair. It's not always kind. But I've learned, too, about my own ability, my own strength, and how my attitude determines so much of what my life becomes.

I'm grateful that I found someone to guide me on this journey, helping me to develop a sense of honor, courage, honesty, discipline, and integrity. Max was a pivotal force in my life. He believed in me as I do in you—you who are reading this journal now. It's been two years since I finished this journal and moved on to another one, to another phase of my journey. Perhaps this will find you at the start of yours. That's why I'm leaving this journal in my high school library, so that people like you might see something here and understand that you have more power over your life then you think. I hope you have someone in your life who understands and who cares.

You possess all that's necessary to live a happy productive life. It's important that you seek those in your life, whoever they might be—parent or friend—who can help you achieve your inspirations. Don't be afraid of a challenge—face it with confidence in your ability to succeed. Whether you believe you can or you believe you can't, you're right!

Have the courage to stand up and be counted. Let the world know that you exist and have a very special purpose to serve. Let the world know that you have rights and insist that they be protected. Be honest in all your dealings with others, including—and most especially—with yourself. Remember that the greatest attribute you may possess is your integrity. That's what will always allow you the gift of self-respect.

It's imperative to set your priorities and focus on the pursuit of what will make you feel complete and not let anyone convince you of anything less. You owe it to yourself, it's your birth right and it's in your grasp at all times—success.

Use the power of your thoughts to create the world you demand. See it in your mind's eye. Sense the feeling of joy in possessing it and experience it now in your life, and you will draw it to you. You're the one who creates your world and you're the one who has to take responsibility for your happiness. Dare to reach for the stars, because life always comes down to choice, not luck. Whatever you think about the most will come into your life regardless of whether you wish it or not. That's the way it works. In the same manner, what you put out in life will always come back to you. That's the truth.

I've shared my story with you hoping it gives you something to think about. I hope you don't have to walk in Yubbie's footsteps, but if you find your life confusing, difficult, and filled with despair, know that in time, with understanding, forgiveness, and compassion toward others, you will be okay. In fact, you'll be better than okay because you'll have a great understanding of your existence and the role that people play in your life. Within you are the answers to every problem. Follow your heart.

I still have a long journey ahead of me. And I know it will bring more wisdom and great achievements. Most importantly, it will allow me to give and receive, to love and be loved, to explore and exercise my potential in ways I haven't yet even imagined. And all that awaits me as I head off to college also awaits you. It's there for all of us.

First learn to love and respect yourself. The rest comes pretty easy. One day you'll sit atop your greatest achievement and say, "Yubbie was right." You'll feel the cool calm air of success and the rays of accomplishment warming your face as I have atop this mountain. You'll look back as I have today and realize the length and purpose of your journey, a journey that was really about gaining insight into your most precious commodity—you.

Author's Note

This book is dedicated to the millions of children and young adults who are or have been targets of bullies. I know your experiences have left enduring emotional scars that lie deep within the very fiber of what defines you as an individual in your youth and potentially in your adult life. I hope you find solace reading this book, knowing you aren't alone and that there is hope. You can become strong.

It is also dedicated to all those parents and adults who have advocated on behalf of the targets and who have tried earnestly to nurture them through their terrible ordeal. Your love and caring may have made a significant difference in their lives. Thank you.

Joe Wojcik